Brian Wibat — not
now at
(I'jacit still)

Das drued with he
Walth

CW00545544

✕

LOOKING FOR A KISS

By Richard Cabut

Looking For A Kiss by Richard Cabut

First Published by PC-Press 2023

First Edition 2023
Copyright Richard Cabut 2023
All rights reserved

Manufactured in England and Estonia

Design by Sam Freeman

Printed and bound in Estonia by Tallinna Raamatutrukikoda

ISBN Paperback - 978-1-7393832-1-3
ISBN Hardback - 978-1-7393832-2-0

Published by PC-Press
www.pc-press.co.uk

✕

CONSIDERED CRITICAL OPINION REGARDING

Looking for a Kiss

'Looking for a kiss is the post-punk classic,' programme notes for the Brockley and Lewisham Literary Festival, 2022.

'Totally fabulous and restores my belief in brilliant, subversive subcultures books still being the active source of our imaginative capital. It's superb in its occupation of alternative realities. An absolute marvel and the writing is just fantastic. Post-cool invites post-punk in the drenched lysergic prism of a novel of addictive transgressions redeemed throughout by the lyrical arc of a prose that elicits lost futures in the defiant present. With Camden as its subcultures locative, and its green canal the novel's pineal gland, Robert and Marlene alienated and unknowable to each other in altered states witness each other's blurred emotions with a philosophic acuity that both stings and leaves astute marks on their dystopian histories. Saturated colour altered states and it's brilliant. It's one of those rare books that brings – via the lyrical arc of prose – lost present lost futures in the defiant present. The characters witness each other's blurred emotions with a philosophic acuity that both stings and leaves astute marks on their dystopian histories. You can't physically meet yourself in the future, but *Looking for a Kiss* takes you as close as you'll get to disjunctive time-travel. A brilliant, upending book in which 'Punk was, in effect, a way of stopping your past from becoming your future," Jeremy Reed, author and poet.

'A Jarmanesque journey in Vivienne Westwood heels, to love's shrine. In no other book could you find Adam Ant and Chris Marker; Richard's lanced love of language is a caterwaul, roar and laugh at the strange turns of fate. Cabut is of the city and more. He strives to write through it. His lines are as urban as the Soho Cafes he prowls. In the shadow of Jarman, and the forever fried Bacon, seeking sensation and the kiss of the cool and the cowed. The indulgent days stoke alarm, not just in the street, but in the souls Cabut describes,' David Erdos, *International Times.*

'The bleak post-punk 1980s. Cabut nails down the Camden street names that can often bring the pain of long lost hangovers and dope paranoia. His sharp confessional and Gaussian blurred fiction (un) romance can sometimes be unsettling for someone who knew, like I do, the intimidation of Agar Grove, and who doesn't want to time travel back to its Murray Street misery with its corner pub and washeteria. Reading this novel sometimes felt like I was dreaming a nightmare together with the writer and the descriptions are often too real to take, but if you were born after the punk rock wars this is an ideal guide to the mood and flavour of that sick mess of time of passer-by destruction and dustbin flowers. As far as I am concerned this is a crucial account of the post-Pistols punk era from an actual WRITER,' – PT Madden, artist (who, notably, was at the very first Sex Pistols concert, St Martin's College of Art, London, November 6th 1975), *The Common Breath.*

'Like a bitter sweet Coltrane solo crashing into Einstürzende Neubauten. Books like *Looking for a Kiss* are a flare in the dark. I can't remember a more memorable clutch of individuals stalking the pages of a book in a very long time. Some of the scenes leave one almost afflicted with PTSD. I thought I was beyond being shaken by the written word – shocked by anything new exciting and original. The book has the same erotic/violent suspense as *Knife in the Water*,' Malcolm Paul, *Expat Press.*

'*Looking for a Kiss* is a brilliant piece of contingent alchemy. To label Cabut's novel as a punk novel would be to limit its scope as a piece of writing. There are rich seams of insight. How does experience become torn away from the idea? *Looking for a Kiss* – descendant of the Decadents... The sex scenes celebrate punk's belief in sensation and are pants down the sexiest I've ever read... beauty where beauty needs no frame of reference. The energy... brings to mind the élan vital of Bergson and AN Whitehead's suggestion that creativity is the one universal of universals in the cosmos. The ... aesthetic of punk took the pre-given communication of signs and made them materially vital... this too is at the heart of Cabut's approach... It is a book that uses the process of creating fiction to open onto a glimpse of what it means to seek meaning through a culture with feeling at the centre... *LFAK* is not like any other novelistic exploration of punk you will ever read... a punk *Tristram Shandy*. *Looking for a Kiss* is a brilliant piece of contingent alchemy because Cabut realised the nihilist stylists had forgotten how meaning comes from feeling,' Mikey Georgeson, singer with David Devant and His Spirit Wife, writer, and educator, *Le Document* (Book of the Month).

'A drug-fuelled beat/punk, love/hate story. Like (say) Kerouac, it's shot through with sadness. Not just the comedown, but the inability to bridge the gulf between the enlightened moment of Beatitude, and the bleak surroundings you exist in the rest of the time,' Paul Gorman, editor, *Into the Gyre*.

'A remarkable eyewitness account from the powerful nihilistic undertow in the wake of punk. If punk as a movement was a single shattering blow, the trick was to resurface, remake/remodel and refuse to be trapped in awe of its hypnotic negativity. LSD was one tool that could be applied with care and consciousness, allowing the author the freedom to zoom in and out, time-travel, and explore the beat bombed world in which we found ourselves at the end of the 80s. I couldn't put this book down and pretty much read it in two or three sessions, savouring the ideas swirling around my head in between,' Elspeth Cherry, *Goodreads*.

'Robert and Marlene are the star-crossed angel headed hipster types tripping their lawless way around the streets of post-punk London. *Looking for a Kiss* is a riot, this raucous call to arms has all the faded grandeur and doomed affectation of your fave rockstar idols,' Ben Robinson, artist and writer, *Goodreads*.

'Cabut's writing is as sharp as any that I've read... his deep commitment to artistic freedom is one that I feel spiritually aligned with... *Looking for a Kiss* is, in my mind, a masterpiece... collapsing temporal sensations in a manner evocative of the postmodern condition, seeking transcendent meaning within punk, acid, sex, speed and living squalor in Camden. Totally blew my mind and ranks among my favourite works of fiction over the last couple of years,' Adam Lehrer, author.

'*Looking for a Kiss* journeys through acid, pop art and teenage perversity. Cabut's skill is in making this journey and the thoughts to go with it as shocking and fascinating as they are. Cabut's descriptions of tripping are the best we have read this side of Julian Cope's *Head On* autobiography,' Banjo, *Louder than War*.

'There's a style and real classiness to Cabut's writing, as he portrays outcasts and outsiders with distinct charm, that brought to mind Jean Genet; maybe it's the way he's able to shovel the shit off certain aspects of life to reveal the stunning jewels hidden underneath. ... a feast of romance, chaos and frustration. We are forced to admit that we are all wearing masks, just some more obvious than others, ' Thomas Moore, author.

'Speed, sex and failure – that is quite magnificent!' @philthenoize65, Instagram.

'This is a book that constantly defies expectations and whose structure and motifs work in subtle ways. The Eighties cling to Seventies punk and Sixties pop art and to a future that's just another spot in a spiralling non-time, temporal and spatial borders blurred,' Ian Taylor, Amazon.

'I loved the book and can vouch for its authenticity. No-one comes out of it unscathed. And yet I admired the mad courage of the participants – trying and frequently failing to find their place in a world that was confusingly indifferent to them. There aren't many accounts of that strange time [post punk] that feel right, but this does,' Jonathan Brooker, writer.

'This book reminds me more of US post-punk writing than of UK or European equivalents... Kathy Acker... Richard Hell... this book is raw, cold, desperate, fucked up,' Michael Gratzke, academic.

'Adrift in 1980s post punk London – inspired,' Jonas Ranssøn, art professional.

'Had to take it a page or two at a time because the intensity and rawness was both too much to take, and too much to miss any bit of its power. It is an existential triumph,' Tony D, *Ripped & Torn.*

'So I read @richard.cabut's very brilliant #lookingforakiss yesterday afternoon. Aside from a style reminiscent of Burroughs, Pyncheon and even Woolf, it's a masterly study in characterisation. Whilst Robert is my new sex symbol who made me want to read Guy Debord in bed (with him), Marlene could be a life-long obsession (from afar). What a brilliantly wrought character she is – living a disembodied, meta-embodied, paranoiac, alienated, absorbed, annoying existence. In spite of this, I laughed out loud many times and felt lots of empathy for this pair of lost souls. The narrative is visceral, brutal, funny and so, so smart. The lack of millennial sensibility was like a shot of adrenaline (or should that be speed?),' @starryveck99, academic.

'The novel reminded me of a more hopeful *Big Sur*. At times raw and visceral, at others poetic and evocative. It's a brilliant book. It is infinitely quotable , it's amusing and contains some excellent poetical descriptions. I liked it stylistically, I liked the story, I loved the whole shebang! Cabut mentions films I dig, writers I dig, and I particularly resonate with his 'Beat' vibes. It reminds of Barry Gifford and Patti Smith too.

I enjoyed that it was meta, the representations of drug taking are very realistic. I feel like I'd get on with the protagonist – his predilection for Dm, his lapsed Catholicism, his interest in the occult, his political leanings, his relationship with booze, and artistically – which adds him to a list a list of characters I've related to, created by the likes of Kerouac, Kafka and Hesse,' Michael John Hulley ll, writer and artist.

'*Looking for a Kiss* has been described as being post punk and pop art but, really, I think its author has moved beyond any such confines or definitions. Having said that, set at the start of the 80s, the book describes perfectly the almost overwhelming crises – personal and cultural – that had to be faced at the end of the 70s, and of the punk era. *Looking for a Kiss* is cool, clever, magical, literary and very, very exciting – the author has found his distinctive voice and train of thought/ideas – it's a novel of insight, wild characterisation, and statement,' Gregory Hesse, photographer.

'I can honestly say it wasn't like anything else I've ever read,' *Torpedo the Ark*.

In memory of Peter Cabut, 22nd February 1960-28th June 2020

Recalling the past is always a matter of recapitulating a reality already remembered elsewhere, at other times. – *Vladimir Nabokov*

i haven't fucked w/the past but I've fucked plenty w/the future. over the skin of silk are scars from the splinters of stages and walls i've caressed. each bolt of wood, like the log of helen, is my pleasure. i would measure the success of a night by the amount of piss and seed I could exude. – *Patti Smith, babelogue,* 1972

A place belongs forever to whoever dreams it hardest, remembers it most obsessively, wrenches it from itself, shapes it, renders it, loves it so radically that he remakes it in his own image. – *Joan Didion*

Well, listen when I tell ya, you got no time for fix
'Cause I just gotta make it, can't afford to miss
If there's one reason, I'm tellin' you this
I feels bad, bad, bad
And I'm lookin' for a kiss – *David Johansen,* New York Dolls

×

INTRODUCTION

by Cathi Unsworth

Through the scrying glass...

'Beyond this, labyrinth and the serpent of memory, is the still point of the world, that gateway which men seek. It is everywhere, and nowhere. It is here and now. Rounded time turns in a circle throughout infinity. In you is the beginning and the end and the forgetfulness beyond. He who murders will swim in blood, lapping against the bounds of time. But he who sings with joy will be continuously greeted with joyfulness. Every deed you accomplish accompanies you throughout time.'
– Dr John Dee (Richard O'Brien), *Jubilee*, Derek Jarman, 1978

'The 1970s were all about conformity,' said Richard Cabut, the first time I met him. It was the June of 2018, which was doing its best to live up to the sizzling summer of 1976. We were talking with *Jubilee*'s Historian of the Void, Amyl Nitrate – aka Jordan Mooney – in an interview for her memoirs, *Defying Gravity*, which I co-authored. Richard was describing how, in the June of punk's rising, he had made his escape from Dunstable: 'a small town, 30 miles from London, where fitting in with your peers was the absolute be-all and end-all. If you didn't join the group of people who were into going to football, having fights and wearing DMs; or if you didn't fit in with the people with the album under their arms and the longer hair, you were thought of as a weirdo and a freak. And you were up for a good kicking every now and again.'

Richard's destiny drew him to a shop at 430 King's Road, where Jordan held court as London's most fearsome and fabled shop manager to Malcolm McLaren and Vivienne Westwood's over-the-counter-culture revolution: SEX and Seditionaries. It was a beacon to a generation of suburban misfits – and for the ones who plucked up enough courage to cross its threshold, a portal into a new world of possibilities.

'In 1976, the world turned on its axis,' Richard considered. 'Overnight, what punk enabled you to do was to look at these peers in a completely different way. They were laughable. Punk rock was a map pointing out possible future alternatives to what was available at the time in suburbia. It did this by connecting the most marvellous things – radical politics, tower blocks, clothes, sense of style...'

From the ferment that produced the Sex Pistols, Siouxsie & The Banshees, Adam & The Ants, X-Ray Spex, The Clash et al, Richard became a writer with a tailor's eye for detail and an alchemist's turn of prose. Far away, in the wilds of Norfolk, my teenage self-discovered his work shining out from the pages of *NME* and *ZigZag*, under various different aliases. Whether he was Richard North or Richard Kick, his writing left a distinct impression: his descriptions not just of the bands he liked but the entire milieu of their ethics and politics, the books that they read and the clothes that they wore, etched so vividly you could just picture: '*A green-haired spike-topped girl wearing a long black pleated skirt, white parachute top and bootlace tie passes a tasselled, black-haired mohawk in creepers, white socks, red pegs and self-made, neatly-designed T-shirt,*' as described in his celebrated *NME* Positive Punk piece in the February of 1983.

The book you hold in your hands now is a wild, Time Tunnel ride back to that formative time, when punk was metamorphosing into something else, a philosophy somewhere between anarchy and magic that had yet to be properly defined. We join our protagonists, Robert and Marlene, under a bridge on the towpath that runs through Camden Town, just as the drugs begin to take hold. They are dressed in all their finery: Seditionaries' Bondage trousers and boots made a few streets away, by the same Greek cobbler that Westwood used to render her designs. Looking good is itself an act of defiance in '*dark, dank, dystopian, and many of the other Ds*' Camden – not just a pivotal punk leyline, but a beacon to the psychotic, visionary and dispossessed from the days Arthur Rimbaud wrote *A Season In Hell* from digs shared with Paul Verlaine in Royal College Street.

The shades of Rimbaud and Verlaine are lurking there, by the old canal, nudging at the edge of Robert's consciousness. Ruminating on his fate – as decreed by a psychic operating out of Camden Lock – that he must never stop writing, he determines to turn his acid trip into a narrative: and to sing his words with joy. '*Beauty will save the world,*' he declares, gazing deep into the Grand Union Canal. Before his eyes, the murky, clagged-up waters transform into the obsidian surface of Elizabethan alchemist Dr John Dee's scrying mirror, becoming a conduit through time and space into which he slips and flows.

Many strange and wonderful things occur on the ensuing trip. Backwards in time, Robert sees the faces of his Polish grandparents lurking in the curtains of his childhood, summoned back by the words of *A Windmill In Old Amsterdam*, randomly spoken by Marlene. On rapid fast forward, he finds an older version of himself living in the New York City of 1989, in the very apartment of former Factory photographer Nat Finklestein, now snapping away at the Club Kids and their leader, Michael Alig, who will find his own kind of notoriety, not as an artist but a murderer. At various points between these weird scenes of past and future, there are werewolves, clairvoyants, talking dead babies, Holy Guardian Angels and a UFO hovering over West Hampstead. Robert and Marlene peel back the edges of their memories and confront their darkest fears over the course of this one long, elastic night of the soul.

I am tempted to believe that much of what he has written here is the truth about Richard Cabut – who, after all, shares many biographical similarities to avatar Robert. As Robert notes at the very beginning of the book: 'the writer, the good writer, is really someone who can manipulate or hoodwink the reader into listening to them talk at length about that strange dream they have just had. So, the writer is a trickster.' This is one of the best definitions of the craft I have ever heard. Generous to a fault, Richard goes on to provide, in his Select Biography, a perfect resource for any budding literary alchemist to follow. Humorous, wise and immaculately suave, this master magician of words has gifted you his grimoire. Use it joyfully.

Cathi Unsworth, Nov 22

Cathi Unsworth began her writing career on *Sounds* in 1987 and has worked for numerous publications as a writer and editor since. She is the author of six pop-cultural crime fiction novels, including *Weirdo* and *Bad Penny Blues*; as well as the co-author of Jordan's Mooney's acclaimed biography *Defying Gravity*. Her latest book is *Season of the Witch: The Book of Goth*, published by Nine Eight in May 2023. For more see www.cathiunsworth.co.uk

×

INTRODUCTION 2

By Jeff Young

I remember certain mornings, walking home still drunk before the hangover kicked in, mornings where the light was amphetamine white in contrast to the shadows of the night and the ultraviolet light of dive bars somewhere in the city that no longer exists. I always had a book in the pocket of my overcoat – something like Henry Miller's *Tropic of Cancer,* Alexander Trocchi's *Cain's Book,* or Herbert Huncke's *The Evening Sun Turned Crimson.* Cheap breakfast in greasy spoon cafes reading *I, Jan Cremer* or *The Thief's Journal,* looking for transgression, sacred monsters, the deviant and depraved. I wanted that delinquent swagger, the night creature sass I found in certain records – the New York Dolls, the Velvet Underground, the Stooges – and oftentimes still it's what I'm looking for in a book, for the wild and the beautiful and damned. I'm reading that book now, this book you have in your hands by Richard Cabut.

I had a friend back in the 80's who was a book thief and I wanted to be a book thief too but I could never find the nerve to slip a paperback into my pocket, and I liked the people who worked in bookshops too much so instead I'd splash my dole money on those books that felt like hand grenades, like danger, like illicit contraband, that felt like stolen goods even though I'd paid for them. This book has that feel of contraband, of illicit goods, of a book thief's pilfer. It feels *underground* like something you'd feverishly seize hold of in Compendium Books in Camden – again, in the city that no longer exists. Those books you'd find in scuzzy bookstores that sold porn in the back room – paperbacks published by Olympia Press, Grove, City Lights, Black Sparrow. Unruly, delinquent literature but beautiful and reeking of cheap booze and sex.

If *Looking for a Kiss* was a girl or boy you fancied you'd call it *wasted* in that nocturnal glam, beautiful narcotic night-creature way. It's got charisma. It's a cool as fuck, beautiful mutant. It hangs out in the margins, in those places where you really shouldn't go but can't resist, the dives and hangouts, the squats and squalid beds, ripe with *demi-monde* atmospheres and fever-dreams. You feel voyeuristically, vicariously drawn into these places, into the thrill and the boredom and the derangement and bad influence of the people who live there. You go to live in Richard Cabut's universe, possibly against your better judgment. You behave with reckless abandon, you become a dreamer with a broken heart, you make mistakes, just like the characters in the book. The atmospheres and degraded sensuality of these places follow you home. You can't wash off the smell.

The book simply reeks of Post-Punk 80's, the years after the doors were kicked in by punk when we went striding through the splinters to seize the possibilities, that brief moment of filth and fury and glorious subcultural, subversive adventure and imaginative anarchy that eventually soured into a bewildering aftermath of dreams unrealized, hopes broken. Even though the book is set in the 80's it doesn't feel nostalgic, doesn't feel about *the past,* it feels alive, *right now,* in the moment, a lived, alive, immersive experience. We drink the booze, we take the drugs, we sleep in dirty sheets. There are vivid glimpses of optimism and beauty in amongst the chaos; glimmers of romantic yearning, beauty in the gutter, a visionary alchemy. Yes, the characters are drugged and fucked up and so is the world but it's beautiful - an ultra-vivid hallucinatory trip into wild transcendent joy.

Early on in the book we hear about a kid who is going over the black lines in a colouring book. Instead of trying to make it better by rubbing out the mistakes he 'tried to make it better by ignoring the black lines completely, by pretending they weren't there at all, and instead filled the whole of the page and not just the parts circumscribed by the black lines, with blazing fuck-off colour. He furiously and feverishly covered every single bit of white, or more like grey, on the colouring page with seething reds and greens and blues. Not to mention amethyst...he had not only gone outside the black lines – he had obliterated them. He now had a page of pure colour that pulsed.' This is what Robert the protagonist does, this is the way he hurtles through the days and nights and through the book's pages. And it seems to me that this is what Richard Cabut is doing here – he's colouring over the lines with blazing fuck-off colour. The book is written in seething reds and greens and blues and the ultra-pink of bubble gum. The language is inky, slangy, hip, rhythmic, burnt, drunk, drugged, stained. The words and the narrative pop with sex and drugs and alcohol, emotional anarchy and ecstatic day-glo derangement. I see myself in these pages, the deliberately wayward life I lived back then in the wild and messy 1980's. I *know* Robert. I probably fancied his lover, Marlene. And I didn't know Richard Cabut back then but I feel as though I did, as if I was often very close to him, we were each other's shadow in the city of bright sad stars falling down from the sky.

Looking for a Kiss has sex appeal and a certain narcotic glamour. If you saw it in the back room of a Soho dive bar you'd fancy it and want to take it home to bed. It's a book that is drunk on its own blood and sweat, its stars in the gutter panache, mascara smudged, hair ruffled up just so, a lipstick stained cigarette on its lip on a mouth that's always looking for a kiss. You should really drain your glass and head out into the night but if you did that you'd miss out on the kiss and you'd never know how that mouth tasted and you'd never fall in love just for the night.

I love this book. It smells beautiful. It's a great kisser. I want you to love it too. So, I think you should order one last drink, chat this book up and walk it home in the early morning light. And when this book asks you what you're looking for then you must tell it. Just hold it in your hands and whisper softly that you're *looking for a kiss.*

Jeff Young, March 2023
1072

Jeff Young is the author of the memoir 'Ghost Town: A Liverpool Shadowplay' which was shortlisted for the Costa and Portico Prizes. His essays and articles have been published in numerous magazines and broadcast on BBC Radio 3. For over 30 years he has written for radio and stage, large scale events in unusual places and he makes collages and installations. Upcoming work includes 'Deliria' for Rough Trade Books and 'Wild Twin', his second memoir.

INTRODUCTION TO THIS NEW EDITION

By Richard Cabut

The two questions I'm most often asked about *Looking for a Kiss* are a) is it a true story? Did it really happen? (for instance, in her marvellous introduction Cathi Unsworth ponders briefly over this issue, and posits that it did...) b) what was the youth culture/ cultural background to the tale, and what was your experience of it – the punk scene in the 70s and 80s?

In answer to the second question, we've added three pieces to this new edition of the book, which shed light on the matter – the 'Positive Punk' article written for the *NME* in 1982/1983, a piece entitled 'Kick', which explains the relevance of that Positive Punk piece in the context of the punk scene, circa the turn and early part of that decade, and '1977'; which details the beginning of a cultural and personal arc – the end of which is described via the characters' experiences in *Looking for a Kiss*.

A couple of young punks, Robert and Marlene, are afloat, but barely, in the post-punk 80s. They take acid by the side of the Regents Canal, in Camden, London. The book follows the couple's progress as Robert reflects on the past, and projects into the future, seeing, experiencing and, at the same time, meditating on breakup, breakdown, infidelity, desire, drugs, teenage perversity, clairvoyance, melancholy, madness, punk (what was once a way out has become a dead end, and the original sense of transcendence has become a quagmire), pop art, primal scenes and primal screams, the Spectacle, time, toilet habits, faded chic, the self, personality crises, the endless search for cool/sprezzatura, memory, distance, passivity, vacancy, ambition, artistic success and the search for redemption. (It's strong acid!)

Robert and Marlene, seem to be stuck in a construct that is itself an embodiment of punk's No Future. Seemingly a cultural and societal abyss, although, personally – despite all the vibes in my Positive Punk piece – I remember revelling in all the No Future pessimism/negativity. Some would say that extreme negativity equals true positivity *a la* the theory that true optimists are the most acute pessimists – 'they are the optimists who have run out of options', as it were. I think this is what Nietzsche called 'pessimism of joy'. And maybe that is, in fact, what punk was.

In presenting a problem – a feeling – or *no feelings* – without solutions, pessimism is epic in its refusal to pretend it's all for a purpose – *no real reason*. But instead for the hell and heaven of it.

In this, I guess we can understand an indication of a deep emptiness so colossal that it goes way beyond cynicism – and comes hustling out of the other side as positivity – beyond the simple levels of perception – like shadows and omens, and disorderly magic.

In *Looking for a Kiss*, I think we can see that foreshadowed within one of the characters, Robert, who views his position through a prism of metaphysics. But for both main characters, punk is a change of civilisation. Or, at least a heartfelt desire for that change. Revolt as a movement of meaning.

Certainly, it's a deep engagement – and alongside the desperation, you can feel Robert and Marlene's sense of mourning for what they have lost, and are in the process of losing.

Not that I think they see punk as simply a subculture. As aforementioned, the understanding of punk in the book is akin to change in religion – and all the psychic carnage that might accompany that.

Subcultures are more akin to children who can believe in dreams, can pretend, can be seduced by their own make believe... until the child inside dies. By murder or suicide. There is that in the book, too – on one level, Robert and Marlene's hand-to-mouth existence quickly becomes fruitless, antic and untenable – moreover, repetitive, and for them repetition equals annihilation.

Punk for Robert and Marlene, is a frantic and violent effort to reach out beyond the emptiness, into a universe where it is very possible to discover meanings – which could and would, in the case of one of our protagonists, sustain a lifelong character arc. Everything is always building towards climax, in one sense or another.

The epithet to the introduction of my *Punk is Dead: Modernity*

Killed Every Night book (Zer0 Books, 2017) comes from Donald Barthelme's *Snow White* : 'Our becoming is done. We are what we are. Now it is a question of rocking along with things as they are until we are dead.' Making the point that in the beginning punk was constantly in the process of forming. If the permanent sense of punk is to be found anywhere, it is in this formative gap, this disjuncture – a blank zone inhabited by a Blank Generation – a term used in the way Richard Hell originally intended: a void to be filled by whatever might be conjured and created and produced.

The notion of reality, the world we see around us, is a kind of process of work of the exalted kind, an act of continuous creation. Richard Hell's Blank Space – well, not just his, but you know... – is the work, then, that offers a reply to the vertigo of emptiness and boredom of the world in which such work has ceased, for whatever reason.

Revolt has to be constantly reinvented just like the life it affirms.

If we don't keep it up the uncertainty of revolt that punk represents then there is little left but to submit to the overwhelming power of administration and management that characterises the fragile ends times – a closed and ossified system operated according to the logic of nothing but business. Indifferent to the individual who feels a little crushed or crumpled by new illnesses of the psyche by a world that's fully automated, plastic, prescribed, digitalised, fabricated, conditioned, phony, sterile – and who is asking for an authentic experience.

I guess it's that so-called, 'irreal' idea of jouissance – 'the antithesis of happiness as satisfaction of consumer needs'. Jouissance as connection to an art of living – spirit and flesh.

Must we always keep looking for a kiss? Yes.

Is it a true story? Am I Robert? Did these things happen to me?

Well, yes and no. Is the narrative an accurate portrayal of what happened in reality? Not entirely, no. Is it true? Yes, of course. I think we can say that truth doesn't depend on facts. It depends on imagination and context. CS Lewis said about truth: 'For me, reason is the natural organ of truth; but imagination is the organ of meaning. Imagination, producing new metaphors or revivifying old, is not the cause of truth, but its condition. It is, I confess, undeniable that such a view indirectly implies a kind of truth or rightness in the imagination itself.'[1] I'm with CS.

Tom Stoppard, meanwhile, says: imagination gets at 'the truth of a person' better than the facts. Tom's a bit of a faker, I think, but he's onto something.[2]

Anyway, the blending of the real and the invented is as old time; as old as you feel.

JM Coetzee says: 'We should distinguish two kinds of truth, the first truth to fact, the second something beyond that... we should take truth to fact for granted and concentrate on the more vexing question of a 'higher' truth... the best you can hope for is a story that will not be the truth but may have some truth value of a mixed kind – some historical truth, some poetic truth – a fiction of the truth.'[3] Again, I'm with JM.

I love that idea of that poetic truth – one which grabs, like barbed wire, the essence of truth – until the blood flows (to be a little dramatic).

Writing is always edited and selected from a cache of imagination and memory, as mentioned – sequenced and altered, sped up, slowed down, disconnected, reconnected in different ways. Public and private identities are configured and reconfigured – pushed and pulled – events compressed and distorted. In this way the 'real' story is disrupted and the new story becomes the unreal truth. Or vice versa.

The best books take us beyond simple correctness, and emphasise or declare the overriding importance of vagueness, uncertainty and abstraction regarding art, ideas, and ourselves. The self is an abstraction anyway – especially where art is concerned. It is slippery and tricky. It is made of imagination, memory and obscurity. Certainties are boring in life as they are in art, and again the best books allow us to inhabit an exciting world of ambiguity. In this, different shades activate imagination and enable allure and, yes, truth. Like poetry truth it is not unlike dark energy, it galvanises yet eludes detection or true core. Reality is a quality of the imagination, the affirmative note of the imagination – in poetry – and *Looking for a Kiss* is a poetic novel – this is understood as the principal truth. And it's arguable that all realities in time feed into a fiction about the self.

The book, in the way it is written, and in its subject matter, is about the notion of self. The search for it. This invariably entails a consideration of the idea of time, tapping into a stream that doesn't always move silently and quickly forward, but which instead drifts this way and that – back and forth – sometimes collecting in pools and occasionally stagnating a little. And we can't contemplate the self, and time, without considering both memory and place – Virginia Woolf kindly points out the link between the two – 'Behind the present a profound tunnelling is going on, an underlying excavation of the self. But numerous chambers of experience come to occupy, bewilderingly, the same space.' [4]

The book works on a temporal and spatial level – the stretch backwards and forwards through Camden Town, especially by the canal where the two take their acid trip, and in the flat, the claustrophobia of which is contrasted with the space afforded by Camberwell, in south London, and onto New York, where Robert later spends time.

The best fiction like the best memory raises questions, creates shadows, brings to relief the uneasiness in us. We are put into a place George Saunders called the 'non-knowing.'

Looking for a Kiss certainly inhabits that place – not knowing.

It is not autobiography although, we're moving in the right direction if we take Alain Robbe Grillet's *The Mirror* as a model of fictional autobiography. It rubbishes the concept of neat chronology. The balance of past present and absoluteness is mixed up via and in the narrative. 'The advent of the modern novel is precisely linked to this discovery that reality is discontinuous and composed of elements juxtaposed in random fashion, Each of which is unique to grasp in that they emerge in a constantly unforeseen irrelevant haphazard way,' writes poet Jeremy Reed.

Looking for a Kiss is perhaps not even auto-fiction – although I guess it might be nice to be in the same camp as, say, Catherine Millet or Amélie Nothomb or Anne Wiazemsky – as the cover notes on Serge Doubrovsky's 1977 book *Fils* put it: 'Autobiography? No, that is a privilege reserved for the important people of this world, at the end of their lives, in a refined style. Fiction, of events and facts strictly real; autofiction, if you will, to have entrusted the language of an adventure to the adventure of language, outside of the wisdom and the syntax of the novel, traditional or new. Interactions, threads of words, alliterations, assonances, dissonances, writing before or after literature, concrete, as we say, music.'

This is fiction as a drift of music, as a dream – which is how it's perhaps best to think of, and where to leave Robert and Marlene: forever young dreamers wrapped in reverie in Camden Town.

×

CHAPTER ONE

Blurring the line between observed and sensed experience

Bloop! If colour was a sound, which is how Robert saw it, then that word, bloop! is the sound that this colour or, to be more precise, this mixture of colours would be.

'Bloop!' he said out loud.

It's a stupid word. But Robert was pleased with himself for being able to express it. He was glad, pretty much all over, to be able to vocalise, to describe succinctly, what he saw with his very wide open eyes.

Which was: - Imagine a child's colouring book to which some annoying kid, anxious to make a big creative impression, had taken the thickest, most vivid wax crayons he could find in the box. But because that kid had been so excited about what he was doing, and because he was only a kid, and a little cack-handed, he had, like most little kids, gone over the black lines. After he had finished the picture, he looked at it and saw what he had done – that he had gone over the lines. *That picture doesn't look proper,* he thought. It didn't look real. So, although he did not really care that much, and felt that, well, in the scheme of things, it didn't really matter – why should you keep within the lines, after all? It's a stupid rule, if, indeed there was such a rule, he would make it better. But he didn't make it better by trying to rub out the bad bits – the streaks and smears of colour – that had gone over the black lines. How can you rub out wax crayon in any case? Even a kid knows that is impossible. No, he tried to make it better by ignoring the black lines completely, by pretending they weren't there at all, and instead filled the whole of the page and not just the parts circumscribed by the black lines, with blazing fuck-off colour. He furiously and feverishly covered every single bit of white, or more like grey, on the colouring page with seething reds and greens and blues. Not to mention amethyst – that's a shade of purple; it was a flash colouring set. Thickly. So, thanks to the texture, the colours seemed to move into each other, as though they were a little alive. Breathing a little maybe. Sliding at the very least. And then that kid sat back and looked at the page with some satisfaction – he had made something new – he had not only gone outside the black lines – he had obliterated them. He now had a page of pure colour that pulsed. This made the boy laugh. He had created, ta-da... art.

And that is exactly what Robert saw. The world in front of him without any solid borders – just a collage of throbbing, primary colours – apart from the amethyst, of course.

And this made Robert laugh. *Well*, he thought, *it is either laugh or panic.* He also thought, *it's a mess. A real mess. But it is my mess.*

The acid that Robert had taken earlier had started to peak.

The drug came in waves – starting with little ripples of unreality – a little smudge to the edges of your vision – slowly building to big crashing waves of distortion and illusion that could, if you let them, sweep you away in the vicious undertow. It was a question of sink or swim and Robert had no intention of floundering.

'It's just a drug,' he told Marlene, who had also taken a hit, a bit of blotter. 'It's not real. Just enjoy it – surf it – it's Pop Art! It's Warhol!'

Marlene looked confused.

He added, to clarify: 'It is... Bloop!'

The same sound a big bubble makes when it mysteriously forms and starts to rise to the top of sea. Bloop is the sound it makes as it, well, bloops to the surface.

Bloop is also the sound that the waxy, gleaming, fat colours make as they jostle with each other on the colouring book they cover – like tectonic plates shifting against each other – but instead of creating a grinding noise, they skim to make: bloop.

It is a safe sound. A fun sound. As childlike as the kid's colouring book. As innocent as his attempt to convert the failure into wild success – a picture of his own making rather than one prescribed by the makers of the book.

Safe as Warhol. Bloop!

The sound reminded Robert that it might just be okay in the end – that , well, he might not be able to distinguish exactly where he and Marlene were – because what was in front of his eyes was a big mess of colours – *my God this acid is strong!* – but that eventually, he would be able to make out the black lines again. The wave had knocked him off his feet – but it was okay, he was secure in big bubble which was protecting him and taking him to the surface once again.

'Bloop!' Robert said, and turned away slowly from a troubled Marlene.

×

CHAPTER TWO

Advertising slogans for the future

Robert peered beyond the colours and was able to make out, not waves like those which had tried to drag him under, but ripples of water. So, that's where they were, by the local canal. In summer darkness, the lighting quality was reminiscent of dusky scenes in some of Peter Greenway's films, especially *Drowning by Numbers* – brim with otherness and the mystical. It was this light which imbued the canal with a sense of romance; enabling it as a conduit of, despite the crap dumped into it, unnatural purity – weaving with the moon reflected on its surface through the margins of something more uncivilised and disorderly. The light and the smell – of shit, piss, blocked drains and something very, very old. The stink took you on a trip and was almost hallucinatory in itself.

He thought, *I wonder if I should mention that this it is all a metaphor?* He thought this because he was a writer and, unfortunately, writers sometimes have those sort of thoughts: everything is like something else, that's the problem.

Or, at least he thought he *might* just be a writer. He wrote about music for the *NME* – although his sights were set on the higher ground, from where you could perhaps see the world and remake it in a way that might be closer to your ever loving/forever hating heart. No one wants to hear about other people's worlds, or dreams – other people's dreams are one of the most boring things, everyone knows that – so the writer, the good writer, is really someone who can manipulate or hoodwink the reader into listening to them talk at length about that strange dream they have just had. So, the writer is a trickster. Robert loved that idea.

If only he had the time, or rather the wherewithal, to write... soon...

He thought he might just be a writer because in his head he was always describing, analysing, contextualising, recalibrating experiences and feelings within novelised scenarios – in other words, he could sort of tell a story. He imagined another world and other ways of living.

... in between his preoccupations with the hard grip of the night, the ecstasy (not the drug), dreams of tomorrow – always tomorrow – emotional anarchy, physical chaos, and the twin poles, shrines even, of utter freedom and total security and... nowhereness...

Really, though, he knew that writing in your head was not the same as actually writing on paper – putting one, hopefully, beautiful, meaningful, illuminating, not to mention amusing, word in front of the other on paper. Not at all. Even he, in his limited experience, knew that fresh notions, designs and feelings came from the very process of actually writing. The unfolding page itself gave life to new words and worlds. *When language isn't written down it is less than zero,* Robert thought, *maybe there is a God in the typewriter. The Creator. I just tap the keys. I don't know. Who knows? I'm not sure.* He infrequently tapped the keys in a meaningful sense in any case.

... this prevarication would continue into old age. Although prevarication is a weird way of looking at writing: when something is ready to be written, it will be.

Robert also felt like a writer because a psychic once told him that he was. The psychic, in Camden Lock, at the top of a row of shops in the courtyard, looked worriedly at Robert. Psychics are usually expert at softening blows when they think they see bad and sad events coming along. They say things like, 'You will be faced with, um, a very challenging situation. You are lucky! You have the chance to grow as person!' This might be in reference to the vision of some profound personal future shock. But Robert's psychic told him straight: 'You have lost track of the arc of your own life. You don't know who you are. You tell and are told lies. You will be very unhappy. You're a writer aren't you? Yes, yes you are, good. The only thing you can do, the only advice I can give you is: don't ever stop writing.'

Robert thought, *stop writing? Maybe I should start!* But, with the unshakeable youthful (Robert was in his early- twenties) belief in all that is wild and messy, that start would be constantly and consistently postponed. A future deferred. Yes indeed, no time like the future.

But looking at the psychic's tarot cards, a Celtic spread pockmarked by Swords – nine and ten for starters – and listening to the way he told the tale, Robert realised that the best writers are like the best psychics: they can tell the future.

He pondered, in simple terms, writers know what is going to

happen at the end of the story – or, if that's the way it is, the creative force of which the writer is an agent knows what's going to happen at the end. And, if writing is a ritual – and most, if not all, writers will tell you that it is – then the process of putting one word after another is nothing if not an invocation.

This thought made even more sense to Robert when he recalled it while he was in the midst of his trip. Bloop!

Still ignoring Marlene, he looked at the water for what seemed like an eternity or more, the way it moved this way and that – swaying murkily; both Robert and the canal.

Robert looked at the canal again and saw the waterway as a ribbon stretching not just from place to place but as some sort of amorphous, unlimited, unstructured time stream – past and future – with ambient undercurrents of subliminal meaning – disorienting but always in motion.

Times flies. But it also flows. *This canal*, he resolved, *is all about time, and being able to see what happens as time, the canal, drifts, cascades and sometimes floods – it is all to do with clairvoyance. If I was a professional psychic, I would set up my stall right here. By the canal side. The canal could be used for scrying in the same way as John Dee's crystal ball.*

Robert thought of Derek Jarman's film *Jubilee*, which he had seen several times for the Adam and the Ants footage, and the most truthful depiction of punk of any movie – and never mind Viv Westwood's nonsensical *Letter to Derek Jarman* T-shirt. More recently he'd realised that the film's real significance lay in the John Dee/alchemy/Ariel/ time travel scenes and themes. These sparked in him the idea that life was an array of portents and visions for another, future life. Obviously, no need for acid, this lad. It was this occult chemistry that truly *inhabited* the film's viewer, in the same way as the film's first piece of music, Brian Eno's ghostly *Slow Water,* from *Music For Films,* which rendered the rest of the soundtrack almost inaudible on a certain level – in this respect it was magic because it made things disappear. *Jubilee* led Robert to think that even if there is pattern and substance in the universe, this substance is meant to be hallucinatory and arcane. And if it is meant to be chaotic, too, then it also contains a strange acumen which, like the scrying of John Dee, and his like, no one really ever fathoms. *Jarman has surpassed himself,* he thought – plus, Robert really liked Jordan's twinset and pearls.

Robert loved the sense of possibility in writing (and in fortune telling), but worried that he might sound like one of those earnest academics, or even some of the other writers at the *NME* who came across like earnest academics – quoting Nietzsche, or whoever, and noting down their brilliant thoughts in their real Filofaxes. Robert only had a fake one. He also read Nietzsche, or whoever, but wouldn't wear it on his sleeve. Paunches, bad breath, receding hair in their youth, these young men – and they were all men – wanted desperately to be regarded as all-knowing but were afraid to catch sight of their reflections in shop windows for fear of disgusting themselves. Looking in the mirror was out of the question. They trembled with fear, Robert had noted, if ever some young woman, in thrall to their clever words, ever approached them. He hated the way they cited Derrida while making it all sound like advertising slogans – they were the sort of who think there's always a simple answer and who can't understand why we can't just... But, Robert thought, *the world, as they say, belongs to those who can explain it – and these guys seem as though they are doing just that – they are going to win.* They, the fakes and fools, as Robert saw them, are *always* going to win.

Or, perhaps Robert was feeling a little resentful and jealous – he had come to realise that his career was failing, while theirs' was on the up. *No, no, it's not jealousy,* he countered his own thought, *it's like the fight in the 1950s between the Beatniks and their critics.* Those who severely judged their work, their lives.

The Beats were interested in transcendence, the critics only in putting things in dusty boxes. In their tiring search for exactness their lives were half lived. And in their envy, they gave the Beats hell.

Still, a poet can endure anything and everything thrown at him. In response, he or she just writes increasingly miserable poetry.

Robert never wanted to be a 'critic' – that was his big problem at the *NME.*

He thought. *If I wrote this story,* this *very story, about the canal, the acid, Marlene and me, I'd make it, in parts, an unruly stream of babble. But intense. With the liberty to fathom all the forgotten ideas about, maybe, loss of purpose. It would be as much a mood-board as anything, one that would affect the reader as much as something annoyingly posed, depending on the capacity for slo-mo day-glo, or slo-glo day-mo, writing.*

He paused.

The action would drift like the swirls in the canal – future and the past. It would definitely need some plot tension though – something that keeps people reading in anticipation. Perhaps.

He peered into those swirls and saw clearly into the future – the canal, he realised, had rendered him clairvoyant. He could now tell the future. Just like that.

Marlene is cheating on me, it's going to get grimy, there will be pain and deliverance, all at once.

It's a true story based on lies, he realised. The most interesting kind of story.

With the idea that we learn a truth, only to try to escape from it. But, in escape there's always both pleasure and pain.

What a drag. There's always a rub and a kick in the teeth, too.

He wondered, *is this melodrama enough for people?*

Ah, readers get too hung up on plot anyway, he said to himself.

If nothing happens, everything *becomes meaningful.*

He continued his acid train of thought: *anyway, this story doesn't belong in a book, as such, it needs to be part of an* album. Robert had been reading a book of Verlaine's correspondence, and Stéphane Mallarmé, in an 1885 letter to Mr V, mentioned that the bits and pieces he had written over the years, 'Make up an album, but not a book' – which later sparked the imagination of Roland Barthes, who described the idea of the album – circumstantial, discontinuous, and lacking in structure – as a powerful form of expression because it offered what is usually left out.

Robert liked this idea – he thought it might be revelatory and honest. Or, not, perhaps. He could see, decades in the future, talking about this with a pal, Molly, who said, 'Are we lazy for avoiding structures/procedures or are we right in saying the bits that are left out hold all the meaning? Is it an excuse by the writer who doesn't write? Asking for a friend.'

Robert scratched his head and replied, 'I'm still not sure. In any event, imagined books may not turn out as planned in reality, so let's leave it to the God in the typewriter – not to chance, but to the turn of the page. OK?'

Molly nodded her head and shrugged at the same time.

It might need an introduction, Robert thought about *this* story. *A long one. Sometimes a person's life feels like one long introduction – when is it going to properly start? The truth is, sometimes it never does. The introduction will have to suffice.*

The thought of it made Robert want to run away. *And if I run away, will the words run with me?*

✕

CHAPTER THREE

Bright sad star fell down from the sky

Marlene was jealous of Robert. He was in the safe world of stupid bloop! She hated him. She hated everyone. *The cunt*, she thought, *with his fucking Warhol shit*.

The acid's big bad wave had truly smashed her, and the undertow had dragged her down into the dreadful deep. She was trapped there, flailing around in the depths, miles and miles down, amongst the monsters, the ugly, blind devils. Dirty devils. Marlene knew they were down there, she had encountered them before in that dangerous period just before dropping off to sleep, tucked up seemingly secure in her and Robert's bed in her Camden flat. It was in that hypnagogic haze that there often opened up a little bridge over which clambered imps from the id.

In the acid deep, meanwhile, Marlene struggled dreadfully along with those mad things. They swam around her, gleefully poking and cruelly cajoling – reminding her of this and pointing out that. The people who had fucked her over, and vice versa. There'd been a lot of both.

Or, the stuff that people called her to her face and behind her back, and said loud enough to be overheard. The stuff that people called out to her.

'That fucking shit Monks single didn't do me any favours,' she told Robert, referring to the 1979 pop punk release. 'Instead of 'Show us your tits,' ' Marlene remembered, 'the local builders suddenly started shouting out 'Nice legs shame about her face.' Cunts.'

Never show them it hurts. But it did. The pain, buried and brushed aside, seemingly exorcised via some retaliatory shouts, settled to the bottom of her mind and heart.

Or, the stuff that people said to her while fucking her. One stinking, shitty punk got her into bed, where he looked at her for a few seconds and then, no words, just tapped her flank so she would turn over and onto all fours. 'Nice arse, shame about the face,' he sang, laughing, as he fucked her.

Marlene. Don't cry. And don't come.

And she took every bout of impotence that crossed her bed very personally. Every limp dick was a stab in the ever hating, always loathing heart. She was disgusted by those flaccid pricks – an insult to her face, she imagined, as she worked hard to make them rise while at the same time despising them more and more. Oh, how one guy ran when he saw her bare her sharp little teeth and bend down to his inert crotch. Oh, how Marlene regretted not being quick enough to inflict the necessary pain on him. Soft pricks are *shit shit shit*. She hated hard pricks too, of course.

Or, the stuff that people didn't say to her while fucking her...

Or, her dad. Her dead dad. Whose sad demise some might see as the ultimate rejection and, stretching it a little, as the most severe and permanent form of impotence. The dad who said to her once, 'Marlene, you may not be beautiful,' and then paused before adding, 'but you are beautiful inside.' Marlene knew that he didn't mean it, that he just thought that was something a dad should say to his daughter. They both knew that she wasn't beautiful inside. Or outside, of course. *Ugly ugly ugly*, that's what her dad was thinking, she knew. *Knew*. She fucking hated her dad. He didn't even smoke and got cancer, what a fucking idiot. But she just smiled at him, like a daughter should. Later on, in her teens, he told her she was, 'A mess.'

Marlene. Don't cry.

Or, Branco, who took her to her first punk gig. Johnny Rotten was the only person in the world who Marlene didn't hate. He was God and the Devil and all the saints put together and she knew he wouldn't want to fuck her. He wouldn't care if he couldn't get it up. And neither would she. She wouldn't even bite his cock. Unless he wanted her to.

Branco was her childhood sweetheart. Her favourite person in the whole world, even though she hated him really, along with their friend, Janet, *the fucking bitch*. They were the gleesome threesome, inseparable. Couldn't prize them apart with a crow bar. Everywhere together. They were one – or, one, two, three, four... after they'd got into punk. It was almost a given, understood by all, that Marlene and Branco, *the cunt*, would marry and Janet would be maid of honour, until ... no... no ...yes!... Branco, tired of the look on Marlene's judgemental and slightly vicious face, left her for Janet. Marlene lost both her *ever fucking loving shithead* boyfriend and her *best fucking cunt mate* in the few seconds it took Branco to reveal his *vile vile vile* betrayal. She never spoke to these pair of cunts ever again.

Branco with his tiny meat. Branco must die. Janet must... Janet with her blue-eyed smile and small tits under her Kings Road tee shirt ... I miss her. I really really hate her more than anyone.

Or, Robert, always talking about writing.

Why can't he just get on with it and then he wouldn't have to bore me to death about it. And his mummy issues. His fucking inability to fucking do anything practical – can't change a lightbulb, useless cunt. Not like Colin. Colin can put up shelves. And he's got a van. A blue one. A bit rusty. But useful. Robert can't drive a fucking scooter – one of those kids ones! And his possessiveness – always cramping my fucking style, it makes it hard to get out on my own to... You'd think he loves me. Fucking idiot. And he's always talking about Situationism and Magick. It's all those books he gets from that shop in Camden, Compendium. Boring place. Still, they sell the Anarchist Cookbook – Viv W used images from that on the Vive Le Rock T-shirt. So, I guess it's OK. And his spotty chest – I told him: 'I hate your spots. They look shit.' I could tell he was really hurt. 'Dry your eyes,' I said. 'I was joking.' And I let him fuck me.

Fuck, she hated it. But sometimes he and his cock made her laugh. And sometimes it hurt.

Fuck.

Fuckery. Little known fact, what's a collection of apes called? A shrewdness. So, what is a collection of monsters called? A fuckery that's what. Marlene was being tormented by a fuckery.

'A fucking fuckery,' she mumbled to herself by the canal side.

'What?' said Robert, who had stopped looking into the future for the time being. 'A fucking what?'

'Monsters,' said Marlene.

The fuckery comprised dead people – or, at least echoes or parodies or representations of them. Her dead dad – who, down in the depths, told her again – one more time for bad luck – that she was a *mess mess mess* – that she was messing it all up – messing her life up because she was a mess. Messed up. Just like Sid Vicious' badge. Marlene got the message.

'I'm a mess!' she said.

The dear departed dad didn't hang around for too long. Sometimes when you hang around with monsters you yourself become one. Other times, when you encounter a monster, that monster wonders which of them is the *real* monster.

The foetuses she had aborted over the years were also there, swimming about, as though in their amniotic fluid. They didn't have too much to say for themselves. But it was the way in which Marlene felt that they looked at her which bothered her most. Looks of hatred. Usually, she didn't give a shit what people thought about her after she has done something to them. But after a confrontation with the foetuses, there was only one thing to do: Marlene slumped to the ground and curled herself into, yes, a foetal ball.

She was going to get her revenge though. She was going to be a star. A blazing, falling, bright star.

The world is a heaving bucket full-to-the-brim-of puke and pus with a sparse sprinkling of joy on top – and that sprinkling is made of stardom. They'll all be sorry.

Robert looked into the future again. He saw, decades in the future, Marlene, a ramshackle figure, white face puffed up with booze and bitterness – grotesque and tragic.

'It's the days after the mournings like this that are the worst,' said that Marlene.

For some reason a Gramsci quote had popped into Robert's mind. 'The old world is dying and the new world struggles to be born – now is the time of monsters.' He wondered whether or not to mention it to Marlene. Best not, he decided.

Instead he thought about ugliness and beauty and how things slip through your fingers like powder, and wondered whether or not he had any real sympathy for Marlene, who he knew, would in the future be tiny and exposed and at the mercy of forces that she could never control.

Beauty will save the world, he resolved – what an Idiot.

×

CHAPTER FOUR

Feelings get bleached out

Back then, 1984, and this will pique the interest of the seekers of untrammelled urbanity and unreconstructed grime, Camden was typically dark, dank, dystopian, and many of the other Ds, too.

It wasn't unknown, in 1984, to come across the sort of mad Paddy that featured in *Withnail and I*: 'I'll murder the pair of yous!' In the Camden backstreets, the boozers were fading testaments to times past, and water passed in the form of piss up against the proverbial wall – and smelling much the same.

But Marlene and Robert were largely oblivious to any of this. They were certainly not poets of the dispossessed. They strutted their Billy-the-Kid sense of cool – bombsite kids clambering out of the ruins – posing their way out of the surrounding dreariness. They were living in their own colourful movie (an earlyish Warhol flick Robert liked to think), which they were sure was incomparably richer, more spontaneous and far more magical than the depressing, collective black-and-white motion-less picture that the 9-5 conformists, or those that stumbled around with their booze-fuelled regrets, had to settle for.

They lived in a hard-to-let housing co-op gaff about ten minutes' walk from the tube, on the way to Pentonville Prison or Kings Cross station, depending on which way the chips fell for you.

There was a rehearsal studio around the corner from the house. There, the female receptionist had a thing about *NME* writer Paul Morley. She sent letters to him and he replied in his excitable, frothy prose enthusing about how he would like to take her to the park for some wine and a talk – about his great concepts and theorems regarding modern pop. No one knows for sure if she actually did meet up with Paul, but she soon became dissatisfied with her boyfriend, with whom she stopped having intercourse – but kept giving blow jobs to. Such was the powerful effect of Morley's words – either that, or she was living in her boyfriend's flat and felt obliged to recompense him for bed and board in some way. A *Slaves of New York* situation – Tama Janowitz's hit book, the thesis of which is that finding a cheap pad is so hard in the Big Apple that people in the arts scene stick with bad choice partners just for a place to live. When Robert read the book, he winced. Their flat was in Marlene's name and his position was precarious. He knew, if she became too irritated with him, Marlene would think nothing of asserting her awesome dominance.

She had already started flexing her beefy muscles.

'What did you say to me? You won't fucking say that when you're not living here. When you're out on the street.'

Then in half an hour she would have forgotten that she had ever uttered such a threat – she said all sorts of bad stuff to all sorts of people all the time, if she had to remember every shit thing she said then she wouldn't have any room left in her head for the really important stuff: wanting. She would then, therefore, be completely surprised to find Robert in a bad mood with her.

'What the fuck is wrong with you, misery guts?'

'What you said.'

'What?'

'You don't remember what you said?'

'What? No, I don't remember.'

If he thought it would make any difference, Robert would have said to her, 'I do.' He might have added, quoting Chris Marker, 'Nothing tells memories from ordinary moments. Only afterwards do they claim remembrance, on account of their scars.'

Marlene would have nodded and laughed a little, maybe. She was not yet at the point where she as a matter of course outwardly displayed her disdain. Robert wouldn't have too long to wait for that.

In the future, they would both look back at those scars and have different views on how they had been etched onto their lives. But no matter, truth is often a malleable concept, and there is always a buried truth, a profound truth, behind the apparent, simple one.

Robert grinned at her – but his smile was stationary.

The house was the shoddy shell of a three-storey Victorian building. Other inhabitants included a drama student, his girlfriend and the son of a famous Beatnik writer.

If Robert and Marlene thought that the mad, the bad, the sad were outside in the gaseous pubs and on the claustrophobic Camden streets, then they should have looked a bit closer to home.

One drunken night, the drama student, jealous that his girlfriend was getting on too well with some South American bloke, got up and went out of the living room where the three of them were talking and drinking too much tequila. He went purposefully to the adjoining kitchen. There, on the rusty cooker that had seen its best days in the 1950s, he boiled a kettle. It took a while – he tried not to watch. He did this calmly. Coldly. It was, perhaps, the only known occasion when a kettle was boiled coldly. When it was steaming, whistling at 212 degrees F. When the water was seething in the same way he secretly was, the student dramatically took the kettle, first putting a towel around the handle so he wouldn't scold his delicate actor's hand, and carried it into the living room. There, as his girlfriend sat on the sofa, the stuffing popping out of it, laughing at some joke, he stood above her – *how dare she laugh at someone else's jokes?* – and calmly, coldly poured the scorching water all down her front. The South American remained a witness agog to someone's world in ruin. Her chest, when the doctors were able to cut the clothes from her, was a like congealed lump of bubbling rubber.

Strangely, her hideous screams did not awaken Robert and Marlene, who had retired to bed long before the actor had decided to play this, his most insane role – one that melted his lover to the core. Years later, this actor would appear in a BBC period drama or two. While she, after botched reconstructive surgery, became someone who looked up at you with the eyes of an old stranger if you dared ask if she was all right.

But then it would have taken a lot to wake Robert and Marlene up. They were still young. They were still busy dreaming in Camden Town.

Looking for a Kiss

✕

CHAPTER FIVE

Happy recovered

'Happiness is really overrated,' said Robert one day.

He didn't believe in or understand the concept – and thought it was just something that was part of a package designed to get people to leave their family in the morning, struggle through the rush hour, buckle down at some boring work, in order to make money to buy stuff they didn't need which would make them 'happy'.

It was the standard Situationist line/feeling, of course. Robert had read all the books – or at least looked at the slogans and admired the art. But, to be fair, it was something he truly felt, too.

Marlene was on board – after all, the Sex Pistols had been influenced by the Situationists, people said.

Robert would write at length, in a semi-serious fashion, about it one day.

He liked the Situs because they were the guys who best pointed out that people were no longer participants but spectators of life – that what people were living was not real life. With no sense of purpose or any tangible feelings of authenticity, they are separated from themselves and their products. This is because, said the Situs, everywhere and in all areas of human activity reality is consistently replaced by likeness – the society of the spectacle, as they put it. Life has become like a crazy, gigantic advert, they said: 'The economy of daily life is based on a continued exchange of humiliations and aggro; the central function of modern life is to accumulate dead gifts; there is no value, meaning or direction in a world where the logic of the market and the sign conspire to suggest that nowadays, there's nowhere else to go but to the shops.'

With a stylish cockiness, the Situs emphasised that 'work was a disgrace', 'the concept of leisure was an insult' and 'real life was elsewhere – *to be rich today is to possess the greatest number of impoverished objects.*'

Modern society, claimed the Situs, is a closed system, which through the process of recuperation absorbs and negates opposition and critiques. It is a feedback system akin to the type of artificial intelligence systems that information theorists dream of. And against this unreal avalanche of things real – Situationist practice was a glorious, 'Non!' to the world of television, consumerism, alienated work, holidays in the sun and 'happiness'.

So, Robert sometimes liked being sad. In fact, it was his duty.

In the early days of the relationship with Marlene, there was nothing much to be sad about. The pair were, to all and intents and purposes, happy. This wouldn't do.

Robert initiated what he called regular sadness sessions. On an evening when nothing much was happening, they would lie on the bed, turn out the lights, close their eyes and listen to melancholic music from Robert's collection – Marlene only had a handful of records (*Never Mind the Bollocks, Bill Haley and the Comets*, etc) – Joy Division, Leonard Cohen, Puccini, Mozart, Lou Reed, Nico, Otis Redding. The usual. Anything in D Minor – the saddest of all keys, if *Spinal Tap* was to be believed. They would listen and reflect.

Robert thought about: his late sister Daniela, an artist and designer, killed in a car crash in '73; his mother – of course he thought about his mother – who had been driven insane by the death of her daughter (and death lived in Robert ever since then, too); and the very fat woman he had seen that day in the nearby alley who was trying to carry her shopping home and struggling so hard just to put one foot in front of the other – shoes on the point of splitting away from her bulging feet. Almost dropping her food but not giving up and the sweat pouring down her face and into the fold of her neck, and her fixed grimace of determination in the face of all of it, every single bit of it – *this life*. Her road must have seemed endless.

It all made Robert want to cry – but it also made him feel good. The sadness hooked him into the world, and into the meaningful events in his own life. The sadness was a black hole he could plunge into that would result in radiance of sorts. He wanted to cry about the ghost of his sister, his mother and the beautiful struggle of the fat woman – and then he wanted to wipe away all the tears, including his own. He hated soppy moralising. He liked being haunted. *Well, it's better than TV*, he thought.

The sorrowful energy was almost touchable. Like, if not velvet, then the cheaper version: velour. Like Marlene felt between her legs.

He always felt like sex afterwards. And he always felt like writing, too. Maybe at the same time. Why not?

I write best when I cry. I write best when I cry and fuck.

He reached out in the darkness, in his head, for a connection to Marlene. But: nothing. He just felt like all the other lonely people who are convinced that their self can find no essential link – or even understanding – with another self.

What a monumental melodrama, he thought. *A right old palaver.*

Anyway, he thought, *it's not about understanding, it's about feeling.*

He felt like he was understanding something about detachment, by sensing, senselessly, the murk outside the window, and the bitter cold in the Camden streets, the dog shit by the kerb, the human shit by the canal side. He caressed this thought of the wilderness and knew that in the expanding gloom every form of dread could be expected.

It's all a car crash, he felt.

Marlene joined in the sadness sessions because she hadn't yet started saying 'no' to each and every one of Robert's suggestions about anything. She hated the idea of feeling sad. It was stupid. She hated the idea of closing her eyes. If she closed her eyes too often, there was always the danger that the voices would start their *fucking shit.*

Dead dad. Some dead kids. Who needs them? Fucking idiots. Leave me alone.

Alone in her head and unconnected. Isolation. *Just like that stupid Joy Division song. Ian Curtis, what had he ever had to moan about? Cunt was a star.* 'Mother I tried please believe me' – *I fuckling hope Robert is listening to this – this is where your mummy's going to get you – a rope around your neck.* 'I'm ashamed of the things I've been put through. I'm ashamed of the person I am' – *that's where you went wrong, Ian, me old chum – no shame, that's my motto. No fucking shame.*

Marlene was shameless. Instead she thought of exactly how she would kill that *fucking cunt Branco. Let's be friends? Let's be foes. Even better, let's be strangers. Tears are not enough – there will be pools of blood. Kill.*

Her thoughts were in monochrome – giving her the feeling and pressure of a migraine in black and white. An austere psychological aesthetic. It all droned on in her head nihilistically.

Robert and Marlene, the happy couple.

In fact, Marlene would have given anything to be happy – she hated happy people because she was envious, and she wanted to slaughter their happiness. Nothing made her happier than breaking up a good friendship. *That will fucking teach them.* She hated the looks on the faces of happy people – that disgusting openness that said yes to everything, all the 'connectedness', all the 'inquisitiveness' about everything even all the bad shit, like... *everything.*

It gave her a headache. Thinking about it. In the dark, listening to *fucking Joy Division* she focussed her mind on the actual neurons and synapses in her head. And was puzzled. Something was wrong.

Maybe the fucking speed has torn holes in my head, she worried.

Or, in her soul. Her arsehole.

It made no sense, she thought, brokenly: *defined in negatives; what I hated hated hated what depressed me, despised, gave voice to gut deep disgust it was a pose but ugly. I am afraid. I am making no sense.*

Something *was* wrong.

They expected me to just swap roles. I would become the best friend. And she would be the girlfriend. Janet. Best friends. Fuck off. My best friend was speed. Like Johnny said: It's all I need. All.

After the big split, Marlene snorted and snorted and snorted amphetamine sulphate until it burned out her feelings – and until she herself burnt out, in roughly the same way as Jimmy in *Quadrophenia,* smashing her scooter (she briefly toyed with Mod) and going bonkers. She quickly became one of those dangerous people playing with fire that other people tended to avoid; like they would skirt around an angry looking, mad dog. Some new boyfriend found her one day sitting in cupboard, talking about voices.

It is all a crash, she felt.

On the bed, in the dark as Joy Division finished, Marlene opened her eyes and blinked. Robert stirred beside her.

I don't want to be screwed, thought Marlene, *and I don't want to feel anything.*

Robert thought: *I want to be screwed, and I want to feel something.*

Curled up unsafe and unsound on the canal side, Marlene realised she had to move. She didn't care about people seeing her in this state, listening to voices in her head saying bad stuff to her. She had even stopped whimpering a little. But her bladder was bothering her.

'How are you feeling?' Robert asked, fairly cheerily.

'They're talking to me,' she said. 'I wish they'd fucking stop. Well, the dead babies aren't talking. They're just giving me shit looks. It's my dead dad, I wish he'd fucking shut the fuck up.'

Robert shook his head: voices of aborted babies – that sounds like some stupid and bad advert for a Pro-Life group.

X

CHAPTER SIX

One of the charms of desire

In his head, Robert was writing this story, the one he and Marlene were enacting at that very moment by the canal. And he was also worried about the appearance of the dead dad. There are too many of them in literature, Jesus in Gethsemane, Superman and Jorel, not to mention tons of Greek Mythology. It can be indicative of lazy writing. This perturbed him. Yes, of course he was lazy, he'd much rather be living in his epic dreams with a reckless gait than sitting at his desk and writing properly – it was hard enough just getting down to his music writing for the *NME* and *ZigZag* – no wonder he wasn't getting anywhere. But he wouldn't like to be thought of as a writer who was cliched. Perhaps, in the story, he'd have to change the father to the uncle, or something. *No, too* Hamlet. *Not that there is anything wrong with a bit of Hamlet. Anyway, it makes sense to establish a main character's relationship to their parents.* He decided to leave the dead dad in, for the time being.

'Are you having a crisis?' Robert asked, even though he knew she was. 'Don't worry, it's common for people to draw on the spirits of their deceased when... '

Marlene stopped listening to him. Yes, this acid trip was a crisis. But it wasn't just about this – her whole fucking life was a fucking crisis.

'I've got to move,' she mumbled.

'Just take it easy,' Robert advised.

'I need to go for a piss!' she exclaimed.

'Bloop!' said Robert.

'Not a poop, a piss!' said Marlene a little more forcefully.

Her bladder was approaching bursting point – before taking the acid they'd had a few pints in the Prince Albert, on Royal College Street, near the canal. This boozer served as a local for their friends who were part of the hippy and punk arts and farts community centred in nearby Georgiana Street.

The acid had now peaked. It would remain strong for another few hours. But the crux had been reached and passed.

It's downhill all the way, Marlene thought to herself.

Robert, too, could now make out ever more strongly the black lines

Looking for a Kiss

of the colouring book. At least he could say other things in addition to bloop!, which he continued to utter now and again, to keep his hand in – and because he knew it was driving Marlene mad.

'A piss?' he puzzled.

Marlene didn't bother answering. She had three choices. One: go back to the flat. But that was ten minutes up the road, and she probably wouldn't make it. Two: go back to the pub, but she could not face anyone at that moment. Three: go for a piss by the side of the canal.

Ordinarily, she would have had little problem in simply pulling down her pants and having a coy squat with her arse stuck out a little, before letting go.

Having said that, she was not a toilet extrovert. She was not a nonchalant or lavish user of the lav. Some couples don't care. They will go to the toilet without closing the door – and piss and shit while talking to their boy/girlfriend. And not just shit carefully, controlling the sphincter so that the turd slides out making little sound apart from a small splash when it hits the water. No, some people will fart copiously, the sound echoing around the bowl, loud enough to drown out the radio or stereo playing in the next room, perhaps. All the while talking normally or joking to their partner, as though nothing unusual was going on. Which, of course, it wasn't.

That was not for Marlene. When she went to the toilet, she made sure that the door was closed. If Robert or anyone else was in the small flat, she made sure that some music was playing to mask any sound she might make. She particularly liked those toilets, public, or in other people's flats, with a fan that started up when the light was switched on – not just because the fan would extract the smell but because the noise it made would allow her to shit without fear – the fear of being heard shitting, there must be a word for that.

Marlene didn't care what people thought of her, it is not that she wanted to maintain some kind of demure, prim, her-crap-don't-smell mystique. Neither was she worried about destroying any sense of romance with Robert with a familiarity that breeds contempt (farting competitions in bed and other such scatological nonsense). She had enough contempt to go around without the need for familiarity. With Marlene, toilet reticence was simply the result of... some Freudian shit.

But this was an emergency. She wanted to piss. She wanted to piss badly... if only... it suddenly came to her, in a flash (in the pan), if only she could piss on *all the fucking fuckers who had fucked with me. Who had shat on me. Yes, piss on them all!*

She dragged herself up from the floor with a sense of urgency and enthusiasm – now pissing was not a simple evacuation of the bladder, it was revenge.

She stayed in the middle of the canal path, not even moving to the grassy side – too much dogshit. God how she hated dogs. Her hatred wasn't reserved for humans. Snarling bastards. Drooling. With their teeth. Fucking teeth. Smearing their shit everywhere – getting it on her Vivienne Westwood boots – or, for a fraction of the price, replicas made by a Greek cobbler in Camden whose shop was not far from this exact spot – just as good as the originals because he was the guy who made all of Viv's boots anyway. *And if I had a kid*, she thought to herself righteously, well, *that kid could be, would definitely be, blinded by dogshit.* Marlene would never have a child.

She did not care if she was seen, she did not want to hide – this was retribution, and that had to be seen to be enacted in order for it to be effective. To act as an example to other potential transgressors.

There was no need to pull her trousers down. The zip of her bondage trousers stretched all the way around the crotch to the buttocks. She wasn't wearing knickers – not for any other reason than they had not bothered to do any laundry for ages. She squatted and opened her legs.

Robert looked on, with some amusement. Bloop!

Marlene, contorted her face, putting her tongue between her teeth, something she always did when concentrating, and pissed.

She closed her eyes.

She let the beery water run out of her body, and heard it hit the concrete.

Robert wondered: *is there anything more urban than the smell of piss on concrete?*

Marlene had once heard someone say that she – *me!* – was as shallow as piss on concrete.

She imagined, she saw, she tried to manifest, the person who said that underneath her arse. That person, Marlene pictured, was part of a crowd that included Branco, her dad, all the mockers, her mum – *no, not my mum!* – *Janet, all the wankers who had fucked me,* who had stolen stardom from her, who had ignored her. And Robert? Of course, Robert! All of them, jostling under her arse, with their mouths open, kneeling underneath her as she dispensed, from a height, urine justice. They drank. Gagged and drank what she gave them. Doctors, former employers, people who had not given her the proper kudos, who had not paid her quite enough homage. She laughed: *the future is an open gaping mouth drinking and gagging on my piss.* An endless stream from a bottomless bladder.

Branco, Janet, Robert, anyone, everyone – *not Johnny Rotten!* – gasping! Gagging! Wretched and retching. Humanity doused in her waste.

Laughing loud now, she muttered – 'Baulking at my piss, whatever will you do when I shit!'

Did I say that out loud? She wondered to herself, although she didn't really care one way or another.

'What?' Robert came out of his trance. He had been staring at Marlene pissing. He admired the functional nature of the zip on the bondage trousers. How clever. Designed for quick access during sex in the bog, or wherever, of course. *All trousers should have such zips,* he mused. And, *she should have worn her Seditionaries' Marilyn Piss T-shirt,* of course she should.

But mainly he admired the piss-off attitude Marlene exuded while pissing, the way she squatted, her legs apart – shameless rather than the sham that usually characterised the approach to her own body – to sex. To having her legs apart in any fashion.

This amazed him.

But what amazed him more was the piss itself as it cascaded down onto the path. Not the fact that it looked like a waterfall. Crashing down. Powerful. Awesome – he looked at it in the same way that people looked upon the Niagara Falls, maybe. But its colour – why, the stream was not boring yellow, but red, and green, and orange, and violet and blue. He was impressed.

Everyone can sing a rainbow. But Marlene can piss one! Bravo.

The froth, though, the foam it created when it hit the ground – that was pure white. Quite a trick.

Then Robert saw something else. 'Look!' he pointed at Marlene's urine.

She opened her eyes and was a little surprised to see Robert standing in front of her rather than underneath, gargling her urine.

'Look,' he repeated, pointing.

She looked down, saw the puddle between her legs.

What was he referring to? The amount of yellow piss?

She followed with her eye the stream of urine as it flowed to the side of the canal and then down, into the water itself.

Ah yes. That's what Robert was on about – *how one thing flows into another. Everything. How things merge. Even piss.* Especially piss.

Ha. Pathetic and ever so slightly profound all at once with a touch of irony thrown in for good luck. A bit too fucking Zen for everyone's good. That is what she loved about Robert sometimes – *no, no, no, no not love.*

'Every little bit helps,' Robert said, as they both watched the piss flow into the canal.

She nodded.

Marlene finished pissing. She felt satisfied. She felt better. Wrongdoers had been disciplined. *Drink piss, muthafuckers.*

'Kiss this,' she said, slapping her own arse.

This was one of the things that made Marlene seem ludicrous, Robert felt – her penchant for quoting Sex Pistols lyrics at every and any opportunity. Finding or underlining significance in the everyday through references to pop songs, or vice versa.

If a friend was going on vacation – Marlene: 'A cheap holiday in other people's misery!'

If someone looked at her blue hair – Marlene: 'Well they're staring all night and they're staring all day.'

And so on.

God, it was tedious.

How about 'You're a liar?' thought Robert. As for 'I'm not an animal' – *let's not go there.*

In the distance, they heard a bunch of people coming their way. Shouts, grunts and drunken bellows in the night.

Robert smiled: in the story, now would be the perfect opportunity to introduce a chase scene. Establish some of that much needed tension: Marlene running fast, while trying to zip up her trousers, Robert running even faster. Knives flashing In the dark. The thud of angry boots. 'We're going to cut you from ear to ear, from here to here, fucking punks. We're going to slice your guts open and chuck your fucking innards around for fun. We're going to jump on your spiky heads and throw you into the canal.' Then Marlene falls, Robert looking back, has a choice... try to save Marlene, or make good his own escape. Tension within tension. Ooh.

But, no. Too crass. Robert couldn't be bothered. And he knew that if there was such a choice to me made, he would try to help her. He also knew that, if roles were reversed, she would *fucking well not.*

'Let's go home,' he said to Marlene.

They staggered to the steps which lead up to the road. Marlene turned and shouted into the night.

'You're as shallow as piss on concrete!'

Silence.

×

CHAPTER SEVEN

Under the thrall of forgetting

Walking up the street to their flat, Robert, despite moving away from the clairvoyant canal, could still see the story, their future, unfold.

A little while in this future, he could see both of them on the bus up Haverstock Hill to the Hampstead Classic where they watched *Withnail and I.*

This film had a big impact both Robert and Marlene.

The journey back was made in silence, the atmosphere one of suspicion. They gave each other the odd penetrative look – jealousy.

Both of them identified with Withnail – the unreconstructed, hopeless, boozer and loser.

Marlene was something of a professional punk, while at the same time working shit jobs for speed and booze money. The housing co-op rent was nothing. Food? *Fuck all.* They lived on lentils. However, Marlene had got the wrong idea about punk from the very start. Punk was, in effect, a way of stopping your past from becoming your future. But from 1976 onwards Marlene was trapped in that punk moment – like a fly in piss coloured amber. No wriggle room forever. Punk had not freed her, she was instead imprisoned by the character she had assumed at that time. Just like her hero Johnny Rotten, who seemed to have, or portray, only one emotion over the course of his whole career and life: anger. Bad energy forever. Marlene's life was underpinned not by momentum but by nostalgia.

Robert could see in the distant future, at retirement age, Marlene – on prescription pills, ravaged by lassitude, mental illness, incuriosity and defeat. In an age characterised by identitarian politics, and the virtue signalling therein, her solidified identity remained: virtuous and angry punk.

Marlene *fucking hated Robert* – in the film he was I, and was going to escape the squalor and waste and embark on a career. *He was going to fucking fulfil himself. She* was meant to be the *fucking star! Stardom stardom stardom.* She craved it, she could see it, she could almost taste it.

'The film tonight,' Marlene came out with it. 'You are I and I am Withnail!'

'I am I?'

'I and I?' Marlene misheard, wondering for second why Robert was using the Rasta phrase?

'What? No... I am not I! I am Withnail,' he insisted. 'You are I!'

A compromised was reached.

'We are I!' Robert said. 'You and I are I!'

'You mean, we are Withnail!' Marlene corrected.

Withnail and we.

Robert also saw himself at a point in a nearer future, only a few years away, sitting at a desk and writing in a diary: 'Am I a man or a slug slithering into oblivious obscurity leaving a shiny/dull trail that people, if they notice it, probably won't even wonder what happened to the slug that made it.'

Fuck, thought Robert. That's a bit melodramatic, mate. Tone it down.

Ultimately, Robert didn't think of himself as a loser. In a way he was arrogant and entitled. People like him weren't losers – of course they weren't! They were, he liked to think, mavericks, free spirits, bohemians, nonconformists. Their lives were utterly extraordinary and enormous and dizzy. They were never poor or penniless. They could be standing in the road begging, it didn't matter – they were completely superior to such mundanity – having zero makes it even easier to be foolish and facetious.

All that mattered to him was maintaining a solid sense of *sprezzatura*, an all-consuming cool.

Robert and Marlene, were eternal youngsters keen to live in a film, overwhelmed by the idea, but knowing that in one way it wasn't real and would have to finish. The End. Credits.

At the start, Robert and Marlene were in lust with autonomy, abandon and deliverance.

They vibrated with youth – an economic design, not particularly calculable in age. They were amongst those who were through, for instance, apathy, disgust, drunkenness and disaffection omitted from the fiscal life of society, and who sometimes saw themselves as auguries of freedom from tradition, family, labour. Youth has nothing to lose but its sense of adventure.

They played like kids – not for nothing was one of Robert's favourite books the hippie ideal for living *Playpower* – but felt like transformative agents, communicating to others the dangerous stultifying nature of everyday life.

They were in tune with their universe. There was no end to their thirst and hunger for desire. Their passion for the world – for *their* world – was limitless. Robert and Marlene thought they could see what real life could be offer; euphoria and elation. They lived on and for craving. Youth is all about wanting. Wanting what? What have you got?

They proceeded to attempt to achieve their dream of complete and permanent personal, cultural and spiritual intoxication and glory by... *wasting time*. They only picked at their art.

They also picked each other's spots sometimes. The ones on their backs where the other could not reach. Black heads, white heads, red heads – so intense were these sessions they seemed to enjoy it more than giving (which was a given as far as Marlene was concerned) and getting head. Certainly, the spot picking sessions sometimes lasted for hours, much longer than their sex sessions – and were definitely more intense. They would go over each other's clogged pores, searching for imperfections and eruptions. That Robert and Marlene marked/celebrated their coupledom in the context of purulence said something about their relationship – that it was pockmarked by the wrong sort of dirty. But picking their spots may have been preferable to picking on each other.

Robert and Marlene, the daydreamer and the idler, agitators and objectors to the world of the regular and the routine. They lived in some sort of self-exile, in an ivory tower. The mistake they made was building it on sand.

They thought they would be forever young, so to them time was of little consequence – however, it was the world which grew older around them.

Peter Pan said to me: growing up, baby, means giving up your dreams.

Being an old has-been punk is a morbid thing, but being an atrophied never-was punk was worse.

And some would say that calling a life unorthodox is just a way of avoiding giving a harsher name to your defeats.

Robert and Marlene, after a while, became fearful about a non-existent future. They were both free, with free time – but, they wondered, *free for what?* And, brutally, they were often reminded that books, music, booze, drugs, holidays (they only made it as far as a caravan park in Hastings, but still...), trips (both varieties), don't come for free.

The couple had managed to suspend and set aside the impact of the unfolding years, the thought of which left them shaken and petrified.

Marlene demanded stardom. Robert demanded recognition.

Both: for what, remained a constant mystery. Especially to themselves.

Outside, they recognised that the world had somehow, while they were dreaming of poetry and chaos, assumed its form of consumer and market culture – people, former friends, everyone except them seemingly, were getting on with their careers, signing record deals, book deals, becoming journalists on the nationals, advertising executives, fashion designers, models, furniture makers, jewellers. They were buying suits, flats, better drugs, travelling to New York regularly. Everyone was splashing around in the soothing bath of luxurious passivity and progress. People were following the cash and the party bash. It was the 80s after all.

Robert and Marlene were still playing. But in that context their play was no longer fun.

Failure became their default setting – and they made the mistake of glorying in their assumed roles of hapless also-rans – you could hear the exultation in their voices as they itemised hardship and calamity.

The couple were drinking a lot. Robert especially found that his centre would and could not be deluged with the creation of sentences, paragraphs, chapters and then books, so instead he drowned it with lager and disgust.

Attempts at creativity barely acted as reminders to the universe of their presence, but acted, nevertheless, as sincere prayers for succour and safety from a future they were unable to activate.

But usually, they were left unfulfilled, unsatisfied and sure that these prayers would remain unanswered.

In their hearts and souls they realised the truth: the blind universe doesn't give a fucking shit, and nothing, absolutely nothing, exists until you yourself make it.

But they did not know how to make much apart from peril and pitfall for themselves. They suffered from paralysis. They could not reinvent themselves or fight back against a dangerous foe because the foe was, of course, themselves.

Their tightly sealed world – an airless chamber – in which, yes, all their ideas were the stuff of genius, and all their conversations were revelatory, and all their jokes were the most amusing anyone had ever heard – but only because no one else ever heard them – their gags were uttered and made sense only to themselves. And in the end not even they laughed at their own jokes.

Amongst it all, the growing sense of exhaustion and desolation, Robert thought they would be saved because they were in it together for ever – they would keep each other warm in a cold world from which they had been frozen out. The Fool.

But everything they had – shared beliefs and emotions – rested on and consisted of thin, rank, stale air. Theirs was not a life, but a retreat. Punk had glamorised concepts such as chaos and blankness. But when Robert and Marlene started living out the words that had previously been written in biro or felt tip on their T-shirts, they found it almost unbearable.

No future.

We are not in the least afraid of the ruins.

In fact, the ruins petrified them.

Robert, walking with Marlene to their Camden flat, knew that it would not be easy for the hapless couple to navigate themselves out from the debris of their own deflated dreams, to free themselves from their own story.

He looked at it coldly, and objectively. The unfolding story. That was the important thing. Ultimately it was the question of what lay under the surface, unknowable, that was so beguiling, raising questions which should be routine like, why oh why must the world consist of a tearing and grinding that approximates the rage and sadness of breakdown, and faded emotions?

Robert said to Marlene. 'I have of late, but wherefore I know not, lost all my mirth and indeed it goes so heavily with my disposition that this goodly frame the earth seems to me a sterile promontory; this most excellent canopy the air, look you, this mighty o'rehanging firmament, this majestical roof fretted with golden fire; why, it appeareth nothing to me but a foul and pestilent congregation of vapours.'

He paused.

And added: 'What a piece of work is a man, how noble in reason, how infinite in faculties, how like an angel in apprehension, how like a God! The beauty of the world, paragon of animals; and yet to me, what is this quintessence of dusk. Man delights not me, no, nor women neither, nor women neither.'

She said to Robert: 'Oh, shut up, for fucks sakes. Just for once, shut the fuck up. Fucking idiot.'

She didn't want to *fucking hear it.*

Say 'Yes'. Feel like a million. Why accept less?

✕

CHAPTER EIGHT

Frozen at centre of the frame during passage of time

One day in the future, or in the past, depending on where you're standing. Marlene and Robert were graced by the visit of Eddie, Marlene's nephew. They had agreed to look after him for the day while Marlene's sister sorted out her divorce.

'I hate that kid,' Marlene said.

'Yeah, I know,' said Robert.

That kid and every kid. But this kid would do for now.

Eddie was autistic, so when they took him out to West End they had to be quite careful. Eddie would just wander off, drifting happily, oblivious to any potential danger that the Metropolis might have in store. While Marlene and Robert browsed in the larger shops, it was easy to lose sight of him for a few minutes. Then the hunt for Eddie would begin.

'Ah, fuck him,' was Marlene's attitude. 'He'll turn up. Look, what do you think of this jumper – it's real shit isn't it. Not exactly Viv Westwood is it? Fucking crap.'

But Robert felt sorry for the kid. He had enough shit to contend with, and was sure to have a lot more soon. Robert went off to look for him. But after fruitlessly searching all the aisles in all the various departments, he began to worry. Robert went back to where he'd left Marlene, but she was no longer there. Concerned, he looked outside and was relieved to spot Marlene with Eddie, down the road. They were looking at something on the wall. Staring at it intently. Robert wondered what it could be, and getting a little closer, saw it was a daddy long legs. In fact, it was the daddy of daddy long legs with the longest legs of any daddy long legs Robert had seen. Amazing in a way.

Eddie was enthralled, unable to take his wide eyes off the remarkable insect.

'Do you like it?' Robert heard Marlene ask.

Eddie did not answer. He merely stared. Marlene looked at the insect, then at Eddie. 'Do you want to kill it?' Robert heard her ask. Eddie said nothing.

Marlene took his hand in hers, and straightened out his thumb. She put his hand up to the wall, to the daddy long legs.

'Are you sure you want to kill it?' said Marlene. Eddie said nothing, just kept staring.

Marlene smiled, thin lipped, and putting Eddie's thumb on the insect squashed it hard, smearing it down the wall until all that remained was a few of those long legs stuck to the wall. Gone daddy gone.

Robert was shocked. Eddie looked vacant.

'Don't run away again, okay?' said Marlene to the boy.

'What's going on?' asked Robert, approaching the pair.

'Nothing,' said Marlene. 'I was just telling Eddie not to run away anymore. Anyway ... so... that shit jumper, I ripped it a little, and put back on the shelf, made it a little more punk. Ha ha. Let's go down the Kings Road, it'll be shit but everywhere is shit now, but fuck it, what about you Eddie? Eddie wants to go down the Kings Road, yeah? Auntie Marlene had some good punk times down there. And after popping into Viv's we can go and laugh at the Boy clothes. Then maybe pop into the Chelsea Potter, have a pint and get some speed. Oops, don't tell your mum I said that will you. Ha ha. And then we can see who's around and see ...'

Marlene talked on as they walked.

People who talk too much, incessantly, sometimes do so because they are needy and empty, and wish to fill that void with words. Any words. But Marlene was not empty – she was full – full of interior voices that she felt the need to drown out. She didn't have anything in particular to say – simply, the sound of her voice drowned out the terrible things the monsters might say.

There is a line in *Jubilee*: 'As long as the music is loud enough we won't hear the world falling apart.' The same logic applied to Marlene's voice – as long as it was loud and insistent enough she couldn't hear herself falling to pieces. She just had to keep talking and shouting.

There is an old joke about people who talk a lot. Someone told it to Marlene. 'Do you know the 12-Step programme for people who talk a lot? On and On Anon!'

Marlene didn't laugh.

After one unfortune episode – for the sake of emotional balance certain nights, persons, events are best forgotten, or set aside in the place reserved for such toxic drama – Marlene went to a doctor who referred her to a therapist. He told her, regarding her ceaseless, sometimes noxious chatter, probably quoting from some book, 'Imagine that you have a child inside you who feels abandoned. This child feels that way because you are not considering his or her feelings. Every time you snare someone into listening to you talk for very long periods, it is as though you are abandoning this child again and again. You want someone else to take responsibility for this child, when he or she is your responsibility...'

Marlene put him straight, 'Listen the only kids I have in me, you fuckwit, are the dead ones – and I'm not paying attention to them, because they are talking fucking shit!' The consultation was over.

Afterwards, Marlene told the story and laughed. She often laughed. Her persona was that of the ever-up-for- a-giggle Cockney woman, complete with suitable slang, all delivered in flurries and streams of quick speech: 'Knock me down with a kipper missus if I'm tellin' you porkies. Nah, I 'aven't got any bees and honey, you berk.' And so on.

Her waving hands, blinking eyes, and her intensity mixed with cackling seemingly self-deprecating laughter. It was both fascinating – like she was transforming dead air into action – and really annoying all at the same time.

To people who hadn't regularly encountered her performance, Marlene seemed like energy on toast – give me two slices, make it three.

Robert liked to imagine that she entered the world kicking and screaming in frustration at having been cooped up for nine months. Because everything she ever did afterwards she did in a chaotic rush as if to make up for lost time.

She always came into the room at a run, the door somehow left on its hinges after she had crashed it open. Or, sometimes, after a few too many, she would stagger in. The booze acted as a de-accelerator, but she would make up for the loss in velocity by increasing the amount of gesticulation or the sheer pace at which she spoke.

Her normal everyday method of talking was akin to hellzapopin': howareyadoing'mjustgoinoffroudnthecornerwanncom ewithorwha?

Robert, or others – especially if they were new to her sphere – would stare at her with a certain amount of incomprehension. She, meanwhile, would grow impatient, stamping her foot

'wellwassamattawidyacatgotachatonguei'mstandingroundlikealemo nmayupyermindyer?'

The response was bemusement or laughter.

This would be answered in turn with the showing of a dirty pair of heels and the slamming of the door that would leave behind a vacuum.

She was like the Tasmanian Devil of Bugs Bunny/Daffy Duck cartoon fame. Communicating via slobbering growls, and indecipherable gibberish, its cyclonic motions ripped through trees, rocks and anything else that got in its way, while it searched for food. Marlene similarly worked a room. There were no survivors. You could run but you could not hide. Her favourite food was attention. Lots of it. Greedy Marlene.

Pandemonium followed her wherever she went. She was hard work, but someone had to do it – namely Robert. Don't mention Colin.

Once, in a huge farm loft in Amsterdam, there were perhaps 30 or 40 people trying to sleep after a big party. But Marlene raved and frothed all night exuding endless Mockney crap. At first there were sniggers and raised eyebrows. People tried to move away from her. Then they started throwing things. She maintained her wild spume of words with accompanying ticks and jerks like she was engaged in some low-level St Vitus Dance. In the end Robert had to drag her out of the room so people could get some sleep. She slumped. It was like the off switch had finally worked on a broken, erratic wind-up toy.

When Jack Kerouac said the only people for him were the mad ones, he was thinking of someone like Marlene, Robert joked.

Marlene loved the joke and laughed loudest. But she did not laugh last. Robert could see that future, of course.

In her mid-twenties Marlene's nature and behaviour was understood, dismissed and even encouraged by friends and associates as being punk rock, just having a laugh, or the result of too much speed and beer – good on you Marlene – or high spirits.

But as the years unfolded any high hopes that Marlene had ever had about stardom were dispelled in a future diminished – what had once been a wide open vista to traverse was now reduced to a thorny track leading to a blank brick wall – the kind of wall on which, decades previously, she might have spray painted No Future. Tragic in the proper sense, her face inflated like hot rubber by her meds, she was diagnosed with a variety of mental disorders.

The aspirations and joys of youth which she thought would insulate her from the terrible damage caused by time now raged in her.

Depression followed her like an invisible piss trail left by rats. She looked like, and had the demeanour of, a half-dissected rodent – cornered and still snarling in her own way; retreating into semi-professional victimhood, and seeking sympathy in a passive aggressive, self-pitying manner on Facebook – this became her real art. Marlene finally grew into the age – a well-matched narcissistic one where everything is focused via the prism of private sorrows and obsessions made public. She became an expert at openly wielding and capitalising on her helplessness.

This was existence as indulgence in specific and non- specific pain, tracing the trajectory of sentiment as far as could uncomfortably be taken.

Some people would say that they had known all along that Marlene was a raving nutcase. Some others just felt bad for her – a narcissist can be very charismatic and seductive. But Marlene didn't really know what to do with that power. Those people she attracted and gathered to her – my *dearest* friends – she later attacked in private as bores, fools, cretins and blockheads.

She cried and sighed: 'Oh God, why do these fucking people, these fucking boring fucked up imbeciles always talk to *me*? Always me! Me!'

Well, knock me down with a kipper.

One day in that distant future, a friend, Terry, asked Robert over coffee (Robert had long since given up booze), 'One thing that has always puzzled me – why did you get together with Marlene in the first place?' There was a pause. Robert thought of a particular line in the Kris Kraus novel *Torpor*, about a character, asked roughly the same question, 'Who sees her marriage as a love story summed up in three words: there was an emptiness. It frightened her. She tried to fill it.'

This was also Robert's answer.

Robert's friend Molly joined the conversation.

'Yeah that's what I don't do. It leaves me very alone, but hey.'

Molly, at a tender age, was self-possessed beyond her years.

'I know,' said Robert. 'You are self-aware. I wasn't. But I do have a character arc!' he laughed.

'It would be bleak if you didn't, wouldn't it!' Molly replied.

'A lot of people don't have character arcs at all, you might find in the future,' Robert said.

'Yeah, that's true,' said Terry.

$$\times$$

×

CHAPTER NINE

Getting out of bed backwards

In Camden, after walking up St Pancras Way, Robert and Marlene started up their road – the flat was just less than half a mile away.

Right then, a rat or mouse crossed their path.

'Did you see that fucking horrible rat, or is it the acid?' asked Marlene.

'It was a mouse,' said Robert.

Marlene shrugged. 'It was brown.'

'It was pink,' said Robert, just to be confusing or because he wanted Marlene to, for no particular reason, believe he was still completely off the page.

He thought of Pinky, a young punk he knew who always dyed her hair that colour. One day, on the tube, someone remarked, within earshot, that it was stupid to dye your hair pink. 'What do you mean dye? I'll have you know I'm a natural pink,' said the young punk, and raised her skirt to expose pink coloured pubes. Pinky also had a white rat, whose fur she'd also dyed the same colour. The story was even written up in a punk fanzine. Pinky would die a decade or so later from cirrhosis. A shame she couldn't dye her pus yellow liver back to its natural pink. Marlene started singing.

I saw a mouse! Where?

There on the stair!

Robert stopped in his tracks. Marlene kept walking. Then stopped, too. She looked back.

Robert was also looking back. Memory whirled, mixing with dreams.

The first song he ever heard, or remembered hearing, was *A Windmill in Old Amsterdam* by Ronnie Hilton. He was 5, and the year was 1965.

The song's chorus may be familiar to connoisseurs of the ludicrous:

I saw a mouse! Where?

There on the stair! Where on the stair? Right there!

A little mouse with clogs on

Well I declare!

Going clip-clippety-clop on the stair

Oh yeah

He heard it, standing looking up, agog maybe, or maybe not, at his parents' big old Fifties valve radio. He was in the small first-floor front room, hard grey and blue flecked linoleum on the floor, from where he could see his father's wardrobe. It was there that he kept his leather belt. The wardrobe door squeaked.

A little mouse with clogs on

He could also see part of his parents' bed. He didn't remember witnessing any Primal Scene, but you don't 'remember' these things usually. You need a Freudian therapist to drag it out, perhaps. The same way that Freud had plumbed the depths of one Sergei Pankejeff, a Russian aristocrat who, in the early 1900s, approached Freud to help him evacuate his bowels without the aid of an enema every time he wanted to go. What could have caused this blockage? The man recounted his childhood dream of being terrified by a group of white wolves sitting in tree. Freud interpreted this as the result of Sergei, or the Wolf Man, as he came to be called in psychoanalytic lore, having witnessed a Primal Scene – his father taking his mother from behind, like an animal. Robert thought: *If I was the Wolf Man I would have told Freud that the wolves were pink – just to see what he would have made of that.*

If Freud said that *the animal must be controlled* and Wilhelm Reich that *the animal must be freed*, Robert was definitely with the latter.

'Wilhelm Reich,' said Robert, in Agar Grove.

'Who?' said Marlene, her interest not particularly piqued.

'A bloke who understood a pink wolf when he saw one,' Robert replied.

'Fucking hippy,' said Marlene. 'It's colourful,' said Robert.

He was thinking: *if you are telling a story, and we all are all the time, then colour is the part of the narrative which lifts the tale from the mundane to the mythic. That's where you find the mysterious and the transcendent, if you're looking for it.* And Robert was looking hard.

Robert may or may not have witnessed a Primal Scene as a baby – Robert, with his acid-boosted powers of insight into the past and future, could feasibly have looked back to check, but the psychology of it all weirded him out. However, as a baby, he had definitely seen a real, large golly doll – 'real' as in something forged amongst the intricacies of consciousness or subconsciousness, which may have interested Mr. Freud, had he been consulted. It happened one night – doesn't it always? – when Robert awoke in his cot to find an actual pre-PC Robertson's jam figure – black, frizzy hair, the lot – staring at him through the bars of the cot. Robert looked at the figure. The figure looked at him. Then fear happened and Robert's screams sent the golly scuttling off to whatever elemental, ludicrous place it had come from. Maybe even across the landing to that first-floor front room, where stood the big radio. Robert, meanwhile, was taken into his parents' bed, sleeping between them. It was uncomfortable.

Robert couldn't imagine why the radio was even there, in the small front bedroom. His parents were not at all fond of background noise, and there was always too much work to do in those days – scrubbing, polishing, wiping, cooking, worrying, crying – to stop for simple everyday radio pleasures. But there it was, the big box of valves, trilling out its mild message, in the same room where Robert also saw, on another occasion, out of the blue, just like that, believe me, two or three large faces of old people in the curtains.

As a youngster, Robert didn't need acid to see things, it seemed. But then kids, before they are told what is possible and what is not, are often open to seemingly bizarre sights. The old people looked at Robert but remained silent. Their grey-haired heads looked down quizzically on him, a little boy, confused rather than scared by that which maybe shouldn't be, or should it? And then, startled by a thought process of disturbed logic – let's imagine another world within yet another world – he ran to escape and hid by a big cupboard near the landing.
Where?
There on the stair!

His mother, who had been busy scrubbing, polishing, wiping, cooking, worrying and crying, sensed that something was wrong. In later years, when Robert no longer lived at home, she would sense other disturbances from afar, knowing when Robert had been arrested, for instance.

On the day he saw the old people in the curtains, she came running up the stairs to save her son from the intangible. These things, memories or dreams, you carry with you.

Robert never did tell his mother about the old people, but she would have known them. They came from the same place as the stuff of the old Polish folk tales, fairy tales, she told Robert in his childhood. Tales which informed him that out there...

Where?

... strangeness and crazy magic were afoot. In her eastern Polish village, before being ethnically cleansed to Siberia by the Russians at the start of World War II, Robert's mother had herself seen the inexplicable lights lit by the village's agitated dead, encountered the devil's horses, and had been warned by her guardian angel about the many trials and, yes, tribulations to come.

Such tales, Robert thought, contain and maintain the unsettling rationale of broken dreams, in which nothing fits, and everything seems inescapable and imminent; and there are always bolts coming out of the blue; affirming that, really, we live in a fuzzy world far from the idea of anything that might be structured.

These same stories were also told to Robert by his *babcia*, or grandmother, who, some years later, climbed the stairs every morning with a cup of tea for her darling grandson.

Going clip-clippety-clop

One stair at a time, slowly, with difficulty, the tea in her shaking hand. Robert, her little prince, waited impatiently in bed, in the first-floor front room where he had years before heard *A Windmill in Old Amsterdam* and seen the old people.

Clip-clippety-clop on the stair

His grandmother's Parkinson's made the cup rattle against the saucer, spilling some of the tea. He would listen to this Parkinson's cup and saucer chatter, and wonder why she couldn't be a little more careful. And couldn't she be a little quicker about it? He was thirsty. In need of refreshment.

Such thoughts! In the same room where not only had he seen the old people in the curtains, but where he had also, many years earlier, gone into a dangerous coma. His parents and a doctor gathered around the boy's bedside, waiting for the ambulance when, according to family lore, he sat up, pointed to a corner of the room

Right there!

and asked: 'Who is the boy in white, the one getting into the coffin?'

Thereupon, his fever broke and he came out of the coma into normal sleep.

Robert was amazed by this peek into a half- remembered dream world, on which it was hard to focus beyond the edges and limits, zeroing into something shimmering and centreless.

Robert was, through the years, convinced that he had almost died, and that perhaps the old people had intervened on his behalf. He had a double protection line on his palm, he was informed by more than one psychic he consulted.

After delivering the tea, much of it slopping in the saucer by now – tsk – Robert's *babcia* would remind him, warn him again: *never get up from bed backwards*. Never. Ever. Otherwise bad things would surely happen. For the rest of his life, Robert would heed that warning whenever he could – if he forgot or was otherwise distracted, he would feel slightly nervous for the rest of the day. This was just one of the superstitions with which the old peasant woman could easily transform the mundane into mystery, myth, and prophesy; spinning dark truths and, of course, untruths. These were her own ludicrous fairy tale songs to sing.

I saw a mouse!

Later, in 1978, Robert wondered if his grandmother, after her death that year, had joined the other old people in the curtains. Those people, Robert never saw again. Nor did he hear *A Windmill in Old Amsterdam* by Ronnie Hilton ever again after he heard it that first time – until Marlene sang it in Camden Town.

Well I declare!

✕

CHAPTER TEN

Sleep meets with brief awakenings, repeatedly

Robert's mind flicked from the past to the future, like strands of his black dyed hair, in a shake of the head.

He saw himself standing in a room, looking at a framed photo.

He saw himself in the future looking at a photograph taken in the past of two young people, Robert and Marlene, grinning hard into a bright new tomorrow.

Robert looked at the picture, taken long ago, and thought: images can lie in many ways, maybe through manipulation or perspective. And, sometimes, over the course of time, he mused, the truth simply seeps out of a photograph like fine-grained sand from between two cupped palms. The smiles on the faces of these two people in the picture: me and her, her and me have long since turned to grimaces frozen in a rictus of ... misery and boredom. Get the picture?

Robert looked at the couple in the picture, a Kodak crack-up. Me and her, her and me. He didn't care about them or her; he wanted to smash the photo to see what was inside; to discover how it works, how the camera's gaze had alighted and then moved on from this sacred moment of reality, now so very unreal. In his reverie, he dreamt an epic dream of an old house hit by a tornado in slow motion. He looked on as millions of minute particles of debris entered the abode through the cracks in the windows and walls, sailing in, clouds of it, to cover every single thing with a cold black dust under which everything reverted to the namelessness from which it came.

So very poetic, he said to himself.

A Catholic boy – he was a mindful ironist realising his small reputation for debauchery and carnality would be both enhanced and dimmed by the cultural and psychological background of a punishing Catholic upbringing – oh, that large dark framed picture of the naked Jesus nailed to a cross hung above his parents bed – from Primal Scene to primal scream, and back again! But it was thanks partly to that Catholicism that Robert believed in the power of magic. At church, during his Confirmation, he was the only one of his group, dressed in his special Sunday best, who mouthed along with the priest's intonations, nodding at the relevant points, shaking his head at hellfire warnings, trusting implicitly in the Holy Ghost to propel him through life.

Having discarded the trappings of that religion in his very early teens, Robert retained faith in the ability of belief to effect change in the universe. So, every night in bed, he prayed, silently mouthing one hundred times, 'I wish he was dead. I wish Colin was dead. I wish he was dead,' etc. Visualising mayhem and breathing deeply, which always filled him with a sense of portent, Robert summoned supposed power from within, even though deep down, he knew that such dreadful thoughts would, rather than provide freedom from his malaise, bind him more tightly to the very pain he sought to escape. Yet, every day, he was mildly surprised that there was no announcement of Colin's death in a van crash, which is how he pictured the demise of the inveterate drink driver. But the good news never came, and Robert eventually abandoned his nightly prayers as mere wishful, and not particularly magical, thinking. But then magical thinking is often associated with grief, *a la* Joan Didion's my *Year of Magical Thinking*, and Robert was at this time already in mourning for his and Marlene's relationship.

Robert had been seduced and then overcome, not by Marlene, but by the comfort she offered for a while. He hated it when she went out. He wanted to stay in. And he knew that when people went out it wasn't because they wanted beautiful drugs, all-consuming blow jobs, exquisite below jobs, bewitching runny mascara, interactions/infractions with delicate people with magnificent minds and graceful sexual organs – 'the diamond grit of the night', as it were. It was because typically, they wanted to effect change in their lives to some degree, large or small. And Marlene wanted to go out all the time. This made Robert, the possessive prick, feel very uneasy. Robert wanted to stay in.

That made Marlene feel *fucking sick.* And tired. Sick of Robert who was holding her back. Why else wasn't she a *fucking star? Eh? Sick and tired of every fucking thing.* Sick of her face in the mirror (she had smashed many a mirror). Sick of the monsters. Of their voices. Of not being *a fucking star star star yet... oh stardust twinkle down on me*, she cried and wrung her heart in desperation nightly. She went out in her glad rags, but often forgot her hand bag, to see if she could attract *destiny.*

The lesson Robert had yet to learn and one that Marlene would never learn, perhaps, was that the truly magical way to get what you want is actually the opposite of the method they themselves were using – by employing not desperate magical thinking, but by adopting a magical *nonchalance*. By being cool, in other words. If you, first, affirm your desire and then forget about it and allow things come to you in their own time, they often will.

But what Marlene *had* learned, after a fashion, was that her experience of love, or a cheap approximation of that exalted feeling (Johnny Rotten had told her – via a music paper interview, but he was only talking to *her* – that love was not for humans) wasn't great. Taking it all into account, weighing everything up, it seemed clear the Eros hadn't exactly smiled on Marlene. Although, she hadn't particularly helped herself. The typical process for Marlene had been so far, so not good: initial animation about the idea that someone could restore her withered black heart – *oh, look what those monsters have done to me* – would be followed quickly by a sense of rage when the chosen person could not, or more likely would not, perform the impossible. And then that person, too, would become one of the Marlene's monsters who, she felt, had used and abused her. So, Marlene was always on the brink of outrage, full of impatience and hate – for everyone and everything that might have thwarted her. That this might merely be some person in the street, or in some club, who wore the wrong shoes or said the wrong things in the right way or the right things in the wrong way was by and by. Marlene, like most keenly judgemental people, was herself... arduous.

Robert knew that Marlene had the malevolent energy of deranged clowns, and that this energy was her mad muse. But he was still scared: of losing Marlene; of finding himself in the next unpredictable place. Where perhaps nothing would make sense, although yes, of course, certainly, nothing made sense then, at that time, either. He was not yet ready to repudiate the succour of degraded domesticity and answer the wild call of chance. He was not yet ready to say: 'Better to succumb in the roaring infinities than *this*.'

So, the poor fool held on to Marlene the way a man who thinks he's going to drown holds on to a heavy weight.

Really, what Robert didn't yet have was wisdom. Which, in the end, is really about trying to understand the complicated sense of arrangement between what drives a person and what could be called ethics and integrity – and that comes eventually by listening to your deepest self.

Marlene didn't have it, wisdom, because the voice of her deepest self sounded just like the voices of those monsters she was forever trying to blot out.

'We are what we regularly do,' that voice was trying to say. Marlene wasn't listening.

Marlene fucked people over. And she always overdid it, becoming objectionable.

This is what the voices reminded her of on a daily basis.

Meanwhile, Robert was always frantic and became pitiful.

'What are you trying to prove?' she said to him one day.

'That I love you. That you don't love me,' he said to her. As soon as he said it, he wondered why he had.

'Don't be so fucking sentimental, it makes me fucking sick. With your spotty chest, and always asking me where I'm going. Corny Polish cunt, ' she said.

There was no answer to that, really.

'But *of course* I love you,' she said to him straight away after her outburst, stroking his cheek and patting his head as she went out of the door.

Both were kidding themselves and kidding in general, or vice versa. Marlene was snide, but Robert was self-deluded.

There would be no big emotional or psychological marks at the end of this episode in Robert's life. But there would be growth and the vaunted character arc, which is the most important part of any story by far.

Robert, in Camden, looking to the future, laughed and thought about the unfolding story he was writing in his head – about how it would work on paper – and reflected: the thing about Marlene and her punk disdain for sentimentality: in reality it is the inability to be a complete human being – because being human is to sometimes be open and unafraid of the sentimental, the stupid and, yeah, the pitiful. About himself, he thought: when they claim you, the roaring infinites are never to be denied, never mind how hard you try.

Robert first knew that Marlene was cheating on him – although, really, he *knew* before – everyone always does – came after a weekend away with his mum – oh, young men rendered soft and inert by the love of their mothers.

The atmosphere at the flat had been verging on the evil for a while , and Robert's antenna had been up – clairvoyance in him was not triggered just by writing, or the peak experience of acid, or by proximity in that respect to a canal, which was something he himself imbued with the power of transmission anyway – neurosis would do the trick just as well. There is a story involving Joe Orton being tracked down by jealous boyfriend Ken Halliwell, who phoned Joe's publisher. 'How did he know you were here?' asked the publisher. 'They always know when they're in *that* state,' said Orton. Robert knew *that* state very well indeed.

One day, he found a strange stray blonde hair on the pillow case, but Marlene dismissed it, telling him that it was his imagination, even as he held the hair up in front of her. Magically, she managed to activate the internal process that caused him to negate the evidence before his very eyes: 'What are you fucking on about?

Shut up. You must be mad. A hair? I'll tell you what, you are hair brained. That is what you are.'

After another weekend away, he had come back to find a couple of beer cans on the table.

'Someone been over?' he asked.

'No,' she replied. 'I had a beer myself and then went to sleep.'

'Well, how come there are two cans?' he shook his head.

She laughed in his face. 'Why are you questioning me? I can't move for your fucking questions. You make me sick. You and your questions. And your spots. And your Warhol. But if you really want to know the truth...'

'Yeah,' he said.

'Actually, I had three cans, but I threw one away. And left two. That's why there are two cans. OK? Is that alright? You wanted the truth. Three cans. Two left.'

One morning, Marlene went to the corner shop to buy a newspaper. She never read papers, but there was a phone box by the shop. Quickly, Robert rang Colin's number – of course, he knew his number – and, yes, it was engaged. She returned without a paper and said that she was going out to meet a mate, a girlfriend.

'Who?'

'None of your beeswax!'

Beeswax! What a stupid expression, thought Robert.

Certainly, even without the litany of lies uncovered, Robert knew. He knew even without, one day, pulling back the bed covers to find their bed messed up with dried sperm. Lots of it smeared everywhere. What a fucking mess. The swirls and dabs. The curlicue of old semen on black sheets, shouting copious joy and potency. An abstract painting of passion made by a maestro. But not by Robert. Marlene quickly whipped the sheets off the bed and told Robert he was fucking crazy, should be committed, to even think that anything untoward had happened. 'Fucking crazy idiot. You belong in a home. A loony bin.'

Robert began to think he was crazy, as though he was living in a Witold Gombrowicz novel, which is typically a map of extraordinary and portentous configurations and constellations that make absolutely no sense and offer no clue as to the reason behind *what is going the fuck on* – Kafka on bad speed – the systematic confusion of paranoia.

Robert would spend his time detecting things which have no logical connection, a discredit to the world of reality. *This is the stupid, disjointed experimental film that I have been waiting for the whole time, and in which I am now forced to act badly*, thought Robert. Nothing made sense. Robert was distracted and bewildered by the plot. He and Marlene both knew that Colin was the other character – but his part in the script was hidden from the role which Robert was playing. So it goes in these situations, of course.

Robert acted his part, but he did not *act* – like an archetypal, hammy Prince Hamlet he took no action. There was kids' stuff, tantrums and histrionics, some name calling, a bit of plate smashing, but if he had responded properly, confronted Marlene with the standard him-or-me ultimatum, his world would have been turned upside down. The future would've then had to have been faced alone, a concept unthinkable and awful to Robert who, as a child, had told a school friend: 'You can't be lonely in this day and age – with TV, radio and music to keep you company.' Even as he spoke, Robert knew that reliance on impersonal communication might only affirm isolation. But, the fact he had voiced such an opinion revealed much about his fears.

Swaddled by his mother, and denuded at an early age of independence, he needed a partner who would fulfil lazy emotional needs. Someone who not only wanted him, but who would always be there someone who would save him – *Oh God, I can't do it on my own, I don't want to be on my own.* He was sceptical of the wider world, of his ability to survive and thrive within it, and of the bad decisions he might make. The world was one to fear, not to plunge into and explore and, though Robert was a person who advocated adventure, he secretly sought security. Without Marlene, he was surely doomed to a ghostly place. In short, Robert was scared of his own shadow. *Boo.*

He was also scared because he knew that there are key points – and they don't come often – when people can take a firm grasp of their own lives and change things around for the better. Robert thought he may have missed a big chance.

It sounds like Robert deserved everything he got. No one likes a tedious wet. But, really, all he lacked was a bit of insight. He had not yet learned that his greatest fear, loneliness, is not caused by being alone – rather, it is all to do with not having anyone with whom to honestly exchange ideas and thoughts with. You could be surrounded by a hundred people every day and still feel very lonely.

For all his fears, Robert would never end up being alone, yet there would be no escape from the feeling of loneliness – he never felt as though he belonged to this world. However, he did learn that the associated feeling of desperation could be alleviated and transformed into something positive by creativity, which is the magical process of giving something of yourself to the world.

But back then he thought, where do I go? Every way and path seems wrong.

So, he went nowhere with his unhappiness and did nothing. His life was one of compromise. Of fulfilment postponed. Of fantasy unformed. Of desire denied. Robert and Marlene still had clinical sex, and he thought of each orgasm as a small recompense for betrayal and humiliation. For, what he thought was a crushed soul. Really, his soul wasn't crushed in the slightest – it was just cringing in embarrassment.

Robert never thought of Marlene as ugly – or, if so, marked only by the kind of ugliness that suggested some puzzling spiritual deformity. And that may not have been entirely her fault. And it definitely didn't put him off wanting sex. It would take a lot to put him off that. There was a French girl with really bad breath and... but let's leave that in the past, or the future.

Meanwhile, the sex would suffice for a few days, until the pressure, both physical and emotional, built once more to a peak. Then, resigned, Marlene would get on all fours and proffer impersonal and cold, white buttocks.

The thinker William Gass had many a smart notion, but perhaps his best was the thought that we don't have the 'language which will allow us to distinguish the normal or routine fuck from the glorious, the rare or the lousy one – a fack from a fick, a fick from a fock.' Robert pondered this while mounting Marlene from behind and thought, *this is definitely a fock not a fuck*. Marlene unknowingly agreed. *Ah, what a fock up.*

Marlene also got on all fours for Colin. But she hated cocks. The passion of lovers was for dearth, as far as she was concerned. Hated men. And their stupid needs. It was like the scene in the *Great Rock and Roll Swindle* in which a critic with flies on her face, modelled on Julie Burchill apparently, says, channelling Valerie Solanas and

SCUM: 'You, Steve Jones, are nothing but a walking dildo doing a good plumbing job. You'd swim through a river of snot, wade nostril deep through a mile of vomit, as long as you thought there was a sexy cunt at the end of it – and those cunts! Daddy's girl! Daddy's girls are in awe of the Sex Pistols! They really believe that what they're grooving to bores them to shit! Daddy's girls are just hot water bottles with tits.'

Well, Marlene was a daddy's girl – but her daddy had died and left her and, worse, was now saying shit things to her in her head, like in some cliched script written by someone with an imagination deficiency.

For Marlene, every fuck was a compromise fuck, just a demonstration of options – she never really enjoyed it unless she was utterly off her head. Giving blow jobs was a trade-off – illustrating that in some relationships, the act raises questions of who, exactly, is the real sucker.

Colin. Or, as Robert named him: 'Colin the Wanker.' Or, simply 'the Wanker'. Robert would not call him by his real and given name, would not dignify him, would not admit the humanity of his rival. To Robert, Colin was not a person, more a dismal entity sent by forces dark and dangerous to cause havoc and mayhem in the lives of good people such as himself. If, for the purposes of dehumanisation, Robert could have given him a number instead of a nickname he would have. But, 'the Wanker' would suffice for the time being.

Robert's friend Terry called his own love rival 'the Mollusc.' 'I came in the other night and the Mollusc was sitting in the front room with his trousers round his ankles,' said Terry, detailing his live-in girlfriend's affair.

Colin was a strange and disturbing person. His girlfriend, a friend of Marlene and Robert's, palmed him off on them while she had fun elsewhere, including an affair. In response, Colin exacted an utterly psychotic revenge – he broke into his Jewish girlfriend's flat, sprayed swastikas as well as various hate slogans on her wall – and then went to the local club where he stabbed his rival in the leg. Colin was a loner, with not one friend to call his own – so, afterwards, Marlene and Robert were stuck with him. Yet something about Colin's deranged nature appealed to Marlene, and that's where the trouble started.

Colin was a nasty piece of work by anyone's standards. But if Robert could have accepted him as a person, not simply as a bad smell, he could have asked him, 'Hey, Colin, what name did you call your girlfriend's lover boy?'

There is a telling piece in Henry Miller's *Sexus* where, having unsuccessfully fought against his partner's infidelities and brazen lies, Miller is forced to pretend that everything is okay. For this, he receives a pat on the head, like a good dog, one who wags his tail in appreciation of being allowed to come in from the cold by a woman who has become the master of his fate. At the end of the book, the first part of the *Rosy Crucifixion* trilogy, the canine Miller howls his capitulation. Robert, too, silently howled, the inside of his skull echoing with despair, like the sound of an amplified outburst of static. It was a terrible noise – just like Marlene's monsters – but one which blissfully blocked out even more terrible thoughts, enabling him, the great inaction hero, to continue to exist while trying to slow down time; to decelerate the solid lurch of the fearful and unstoppable future.

Robert was looking at himself looking at photograph of two young people, Robert and Marlene, grinning hard into a bright new tomorrow.

He will in the future think: *this story is an ode to growing pains of eternal children.*

He will think: *this story is about gaining the wherewithal to write your own narrative.*

The story is about attaining the capacity and joy of moving on, and of keeping on moving.

×

CHAPTER ELEVEN

Speed is frozen

Looking for a Kiss

Robert, in Camden, was still looking into the future, and saw himself in a few years' time.

He was living in Camberwell, in south east London. Robert and Marlene were no longer living together, but they were still a couple. Or, pretending to be. Marlene – she had still not achieved stardom – *fucking cunts all of them* – was also seeing Colin. She lied to Robert about doing so. And he pretended to believe her in order to maintain the status quo – he *still* wasn't ready to face the world entirely on his own.

He lived with friends in a big house in Camberwell – a much more free and expansive place than Camden, he felt. He loved the openness and possibility for interaction on offer there. Comparatively, Camden was claustrophobic bedsit land. Camberwell could sometimes, at least, be rinsed in sweeps of allure – Camden was mostly sullen and a little sinister. In Camberwell, Robert played music, read books in the nearby Ruskin Park, wrote for the music papers, took speed, cycled around, saw girls and went about the tricky business of activating the next phase of his life – *this* was far more arousing than the simple search for sex.

He hooked up with Marlene most weekends, to take speed.

Other times, Robert was left to his own debauched devices.

Robert in Camden watched himself in the future in Camberwell, sitting at his desk writing in a large blue diary. He looked over his own shoulder and saw these words, about a drug experience, being written by himself:-

Diary entry 5 June 1988: I tremble and wonder as I cut up some speed. Fix some water in a spoon and mash the mixture into a dangerous solution. Add a piece of fag filter to trap the clag and draw up the watery drug into the needle. Slowly to avoid air bubbles but not quite succeeding and not quite fucking it up enough to start again. Flex my arm with a guitar strap and decide on a thin but prominent vein. Slide the needle in and draw blood – I'm in! Inject the drug, but in my fear of a beginner I shake the needle out of the vein and a bulbous blue swelling arises. I stop in time and start the whole ritual again. On the other arm choosing the big vein. I hear it pop and see the blood and taste the exhilaration as I again, shakily, push the plunger home. There's no real buzz, but I pace the room and smoke fag after fag and find the Johnny Thunders record and play Looking for a Kiss. *For a junkie Thunders plays pretty good amphetamine accompaniments. Feel panicky about not getting a big rush, not really exploding with the drug and dab a whole lot more. And off to meet people at the Cambridge. I am affable and interested. Discharging the night with my spunk into a girl. But where is mention of my career success? My creativity? My financial spirit? Nowhere. Elsewhere in a parallel universe. Not here.*

Home next day to read Kentucky Ham. *A tale of an A head jerked out of his self-destructive, needle fixed lifestyle by the authorities and his rehab through work and exertion. I liked the bit where he had four days to go before a deadline and went off the straight and narrow narrative bunging in crumby half-baked quarter thoughts. The book is real, even if as a train of thought it's rubbish – just like this diary.*

Robert, in Camden, was able to see his future self writing about himself in his diary *and* those events being written about, all at the same time. Quite a trick.

But watching himself in this way didn't detract from the concrete composition, depiction and understanding of the scene. It hit Robert like a smack in the eye – or, rather, speed in the eye. Robert's gaze was not at all detached or diluted by time's unfathomable distance.

He thought: it is beautiful but repugnant – and banal, of course. He wished he could take a photograph – the scene might make a good book cover. Art in the aesthetic sense – taut, narcissistic, sinuous, glam and sexual, focused on a silver otherness. Art that challenged perception of, at source, disappearance, nothingness. Art and speed – the underground, underworld pallor and pose of decadence. Robert, in all his temporal positions, was something through which that idea passed.

I need a fix and a kiss
I need a fix and a kiss
I need a fix and a kiss
I been looking for a kiss

Robert thought: *I am not looking for a fix. I want be fixed. The*

Dolls weren't singing about drugs at all – they were singing about fucking redemption.

Robert had never seen himself concentrate on something so intensely as when putting the point of the needle to its target. The vein reminded him of the Camden canal, snaking and foreseeing a future. He thought about the serenity at that very point – *what's the point*? The lack of an initial rush did not surprise him – somehow that lack was apt in context of the aesthetic: distant but electrified. There, in that pressurised gap between desire and insouciance was located the sense of cool that Robert had always cultivated and projected – like a film: *noir*. *But*, he wondered, *is there anything human here*?

Robert watching the scene and himself write about it felt as though he was blurring the line between observed and sensed experience. Amaranthine time. He felt the heartbeat – at the speed of the clock, the speed of his cock, the speed of speed. Context abridged within place and time. Cool collapsed, emotions within amplified imagination. Reclining into the deterioration, digging the vein, digging the/a girl – or, thought of the/a girl. Elegant cold gratification in nothing – but the deep interest in a strangeness of which, in the howling infinites, we are constituted.

Diary entry 11 June, 1988. Saturday and fucked myself up – and fucked Marlene after licking her arsehole and the join of her buttocks and back as though it was her clit. The speed dampened me and I became hard in her very hot cunt before fucking her. The sex isn't as full of wild abandon as it used to be – soon there will be nothing left for us.

Terry talked about girls, Carol – how he'd had trouble with relationships and sex, nothing in bed, how it wouldn't happen for him.

Ray – impotence.

Everyone I know seems to get it together only now and then.

Diary entry 18 June, 1988. The speedy pseudo interest in everything and everybody. The self-assurance. The confidence. All false – shattered by the coming of dawn.

Ah and the lust –I just wanted to stick my cock in the cutie with the black dress – her cunt, mouth and arse. Made do with Marlene. I stick my cock in her mouth and she bites it, I suck and chew her nipples for ages while holding a handful of her hair. Stick a tennis racket up her cunt and finish her off by flicking my tongue over her open cunt while she wanks and licks my asshole. Deep deserved sleep follows. Marlene has to get up early. I sleep and stay in bed until three.

Diary entry 25 June, 1988. At someone's house. We put the double sofa bed out in the front room . Got some alcohol from Graham. Marlene talked to me for ages with speed exhilaration. I listened with speed induced interest. Passing comments and adding opinions. Marlene asked me not to launch into fucking too quickly and to let it come. I held onto her toes, stroked her legs. Then moved onto her tits and actually got her moaning with pleasure. Shock. Moved down to her cunt and licked that but not for too long. Back to her tits which I fucked with my cock. Shoving it in her mouth. Finally getting it in her cunt and riding her. We talked pantingly about how she'd treat a girl. Would she suck her cunt and arse? Yes. Moan. Do I know such a girl? Yes. Would you piss on her? Yes – would you like me to piss on you? No, but I'll piss over your tits and never mind the carpet! She laid herself on the floor as I tried to get the shower to flow. No luck (not getting it up is one thing – but this was the first time not being able to piss! Never happened before, honest). I put an empty vodka bottle into her cunt and went to drink some water. But tired of piss inaction she leapt up stood astride me and let it flow. Smearing her piss over my chest. My turn came, I sat astride her and between her gasps of excitement I splashed her tits. She grabbed my cock and directed it onto her nipples. She looked shy, aghast and exhilarated at the same time. Afterwards I told her she looked like a shy whore. I took her by the nipples and led her to the bed where I fucked and her mouthed more lesbian fantasies as she shuddered and came. I pushed her legs back over her head so that her legs rested on her shoulders and fucked her hard. Her hand fondled my bollocks. I came in gouts. Sleep was sound. Morning – jovial references to pissing.

The film of these scenes would be full of faces, shot in relentless close-ups – all margins and edges; her: tweaked repression; him: unclenched urgency.

Robert, the one being secretly observed by himself, felt weird: like he was being haunted. There was definitely a presence. He had a sense of foreboding. There was a ghost here: a ghost of a chance.

Robert, the observer, believed, like Jacques Derrida, that that the future was full of ghosts – it belonged to ghosts – to the apparitions and those they haunted with their images.

Robert looked at the scene, and thought it was unusual for Marlene to be so present and so intensely immersed. Typically, he thought of Marlene as someone who, by being part of the pre-porn generation, had missed her natural milieu. She was someone who hated sex with men so, *a la* the porn generation, was happy to be fucked any way you/they liked, faking it just like she faked everything: with a rabid vigour – especially her orgasms. She made those into a celebrity/star event, but felt nothing. Like porn, this performative sex was boring – although Marlene treated it as a useful rehearsal for the wider empty spirited performance, on which the function of stardom, and the craving for it, is based.

She would stop having sex relatively early in life after hopes and dreams of even any approximation of stardom had finally been discarded. Colin, who she married, didn't care – it wasn't his thing either. When someone asked her why she married him, Marlene said she needed a new father – someone who would look after her without hurting her feelings. Without saying shit things to her. Like every *fucking* body had, *every fucking cunt has*. What a mess.

Robert thought the scene would also make part of an interesting film. Warhol – of course – came to mind. Robert thought, flippantly, his balls could be like Andy's silver helium balloons – made by Andy so he could watch his career floating away, although of course, it didn't. Robert would offer his balls as a statement of intent – of the auteur, someone with an awareness of his own gestalt rather than just his output . He might paint them silver. Or, write a message on them – in small text, on which the camera would zoom, left and right respectively: 'nothing' and 'emptiness'.

The camera would focus on the scene in mute fascination.

The irony would be seen in Marlene kissing those balls. Marlene who wanted so desperately, more than anything, to be Edie Sedgewick. She empathised with her fucked-up daddy issues – Edie had famously walked in on her adulterous father in bed with a girlfriend and, for her trouble, was slapped by daddy who told her in no uncertain terms that *she did not see what she saw*. Edie's father also made advances on her. Marlene wanted to step into Edie's persona: skinny, stylish, beautiful, cool, rich, a superstar for the sake of it, and in love with self-destruction – all of which, apart from the latter, was unattainable and impossible for her.

Robert felt that he would like to stand, watch and film Marlene as she destroyed herself – with drugs, resentment, jealousy, hate, self-loathing, crime, and self-pity. He would not help, just record the story as it unfolded – his aloof creativity would excuse him from accusations of callous exploitation. Yes, just like Andy.

Robert thought, this film is about art, sex, and speed. And time. The skinny: picture and action streams and leaks, visual isolation curious enthrallment beyond image and attraction – subverted and fixed hallucination – imagined literal time – temporal senselessness and helplessness created by the meaning: sorry, some other time – frustration carnal and obscene: poetry. Yeah.

Robert had it all worked out. A sure fire hit.

The theme of voyeurism, and meditation on same, was a given. Robert, storyteller and self-described auteur, would while watching, not miss a single detail.

Robert finished watching both himself writing about the scene and the scene itself, and concluded: 'My vision and my cock were always clean – what more can anyone ask for?'

CHAPTER TWELVE

The animal must be freed

In Camden, Robert saw himself at the end of the decade, in New York.

Nat Finkelstein's unpublished autobiography, *14 Ounce Pound*, begins with Nat sitting in a prison cell talking to the ghost of his dead father. Nat tries to explain and justify why and how he ended up behind bars (in fact, drug smuggling in Paris); how he traipsed for years around the dusty corners of the globe 'on the run' from US authorities who he believed had put out a 'dead or alive' on him – in fact, this may not have actually been fact – *para-fucking-noia Nat*; how he had been done bad by Andy Warhol; and how he had then taken revenge on the middle class fools, fakes and soft heads, which is also how he viewed the Warhol milieu, by selling drugs – Al Aronowitz described him as, 'Nat Finkelstein, Kokaine King of Woodstock.' The reader isn't told what Nat's dead dad thought of all this. Perhaps he gave him a stiff talking to.

Robert read this work-in-progress while staying with Nat in New York over the summer of '89. He'd interviewed him in the Spring about his book *Andy Warhol: The Factory Years*. He inscribed it: 'To Robert, remember the cry of the mutant, 'I need creatures who resemble me.'' And then kept ringing him to insist he go stay with him in the States – the mutant obviously thought Robert was his kind of creature.

Robert loved that book. A fantastic collection of pictures and memories of the Silver Factory during Finkelstein's tenure as unofficial resident photographer between 1964 and 1967. A chronicle of speed, madness and fabulous art, full of speed freaks, hustlers, junkies and geniuses; recalibrated fantasies about instant celebrity (Nat, by the way, thought Edie was an idiot), money, decadence and rock 'n' roll (Nat's picture featured on the back of the first Velvet Underground LP). Robert's kind of scene.

Nat lived in a tiny first apartment a few blocks across from the East Village. No kitchen. Not even a kettle. If you wanted a coffee, you went downstairs and across the road to the deli. Nat slept in the living room, on a fold out sofa. Robert was in a little annex, with just about room enough for a single bed. When he was with girls, Robert had to go to theirs'. There was no other furniture, and Nat had no possessions to speak of. A suitcase. Some documents – his work-in-progress – and a bunch of old negs (treasure), all just piled up on the floor. A tape player with a couple of cassettes – *London Calling* and *The Velvet Underground* (Robert and Nat discussed which was best – Nat's theory: Brits always went for *VU*, Americans, including himself, the Clash. Yeah, Robert went for *VU*). Nat later topped up this sparse collection after someone he vaguely knew jumped out of the window at the Chelsea Hotel – they went up to the poor soul's room to rifle through his things – so it went in these hurried visits to locations of despair and violence.

There was also a telephone at Nat's. But no one ever rang.

By the turn of the century, art, music, and cultural output of various hues has been flattened and marked down for fast turnaround; packaged, bundled up, repackaged again to satisfy the need for product and the media's requirement for subject matter: boiled down into palatable mulch.

Nat, via his intimate association with Warhol and VU (who he called: 'The psychopath's Rolling Stones'), would, if he had lived, be clamoured over for exhibitions, appearances, interviews, work, rights, prints sales, adverts, the whole shebang.

But in 1989, pre-cultural acceleration, no one really wanted to know. The mutant largely cried in vain.

The phone also never rang because Nat wasn't a particularly well-liked man. He was garrulous, argumentative, gruff, unreconstructed and didn't tread lightly on anyone's sensibilities.

Moreover, he didn't look the part. At the Factory, a world inhabited by beautiful if disposable wild boys and girls, Nat – a small, balding, old-looking schlub – lowered the tone. Lou Reed said, 'The three worst people in the world are Nat Finkelstein and two speed dealers.' Nat was expelled from the Factory paradise when he dared suggest to Andy that they collaborate.

In 1989, Nat was regarded in a similar fashion by the NY Club Kids, whose energy he tried to tap by photographing them in clubs like Red Zone, World, Save the Robots *et al.*

Robert hung out with some of the cooler Clubs Kids, the girls in big platforms, walking to the Chelsea, telling the drug dealers to fuck off.

The Kids, led by future murderer Michael Alig (one of the most truly empty people Robert ever met) tolerated Nat, but only barely, because he had a camera – of course, exposure was something the Kids craved even more than the ketamine and E that fuelled the scene.

The phone remained silent.

But there was a lot to like about Nat, apart from when he had just been freebasing (a former addict, he hadn't quite lost his love of coke at that time).

These were days of E and coke – speed was infra dig and unavailable outside of a bathtub in the Midwest, something Robert was a little sad about.

Yes, Nat was bitter and whiny about his lack of acclaim and respect, but he was also honest about the part he played in his own downfall and stasis via the dismal drugs 'n' crime process.

It was in New York, and via Nat, that Robert finally learned and assimilated the big secret about ambition, creativity and career.

Nat taught him that, well, all considered, in truth, everything flows away sooner or later in an ephemeral kind of way – it is better to shine within the moment, perhaps; to fully fill one's boots and be true to your own nature rather than lick the world's arse.

Robert never forgot and never looked back.

Nat was also courageous – when one of the gang was mugged for his sunglasses outside the opening of a new club on the borders of Alphabet City Nat didn't hesitate in throwing his fair share of punches – he was old school Brooklyn tough. He was funny with it. The writing in the version of *14 Ounce Pound* that Robert read was a little sentimental and maudlin, but his words in *The Factory Years* cut to the quick with a hilarious edge.

Of course, Nat embodied all the acerbity and anguish of the city. His world was tainted with an isolating sense of melancholy, pungency and the fidgety foreboding that it was all going to end in salty tears. But he remained an insouciant outsider following his own crazy rationale – the ambiguous somewhere between elation of expectation and the riddle of failure. And he did it very bluntly, which, again was funny – it was a guffaw in acknowledgement of the mad persistence that keeps everyone all hanging on despite the knocks.

The trip climaxed with a night for Nat's book at the Red Zone club, 440 W 54. The flyer and poster listed those luminaries who organiser, Club Kid Susan Anton, had invited to the event – Betsey Johnson, Coca Crystal, Steve Maas, Herbert Hunke, Mary Woronov, David Dalton, Henry Connell (*Interview*), Gregory Corso and... Robert!

When the summer was over, Robert saw himself return from New York filled with a sense of possibility and the future.

×

CHAPTER THIRTEEN

Tongues – not giving but speaking

Looking for a Kiss

Back in the past, Robert scratched his spikey head.

'What the fuck is that?' he said, looking out of the window.

He and Marlene were in their tiny room in a housing association house in West Hampstead. Before their move to Camden, they shared this house with Robert's friend Terry, a drug fiend called Ziggy and a couple of wannabe fashion designers. Everyone in this scene was a wannabe of sorts – wannabe journalist/writer, rock star, etc. Although, they told themselves, and took pride in the assertion, that unlike, say, the similarly disposed New Romantics they weren't trying to climb up the greasy ladder. They, the last punks, the positive punks, the hippy punks, the true punks, didn't want to ascend the ladder, they wanted to kick it down. They were not careerists, they said. In truth, most would clamber over their crippled auntie to get up that ladder.

Robert and Marlene had been out briefly to the Tribe Club, or it might have been the Batcave, but had left very early.

'What?' said Marlene.

'*That!*' exclaimed Robert, pointing into the night. 'What?'

'Look!'

Marlene joined him at the window and looked at his pointing finger – she clearly had not come across the Zen analogy: 'A finger pointing at the moon is not the moon.' Neither had Robert but he had seen *Enter the Dragon*, in which Bruce Lee pretends to be wise by ripping off that snippet of Buddhist teaching: 'Don't think. FEEEEEEEEL! It's like a finger pointing away to the moon. Do not concentrate on the finger or you will miss all of the heavenly glory!' Bruce is very kindly instructing someone about the importance of staying fully present in the moment. Not drifting off. Drifting off was one of the things that both Robert and Marlene were good at, but not on this night.

'Do you see it?' asked Robert.

'What?' said Marlene, getting a little irritated. '*That!*' Robert gestured with his finger. '*That!*'

What Robert saw in the night sky – *that* – could be most easily described as a UFO. But it wasn't a flying saucer in shape, it wasn't some obscure light in the sky that could be practically anything, it wasn't a cylinder, or a triangle – both common UFO shapes – it was more like the freaking Mothership. It looked like a huge ocean liner floating in the sky, one that could accommodate thousands of people. Or beings. It was marked by rows of brightly lit portholes, from which these beings were, doubtless, Robert imagined, looking down on *him*. It moved slowly, almost imperceptibly so, across the sky, not too high, not too low. No one could miss this, thought Robert.

Finally, Marlene looked up.

'Do you see it?' Robert asked.

Marlene didn't answer, her jaw dropped open. It took something very unusual to stop Marlene talking. Her stunned silence confirmed to Robert that he was not just seeing things. Or, that they had a shared vision, perhaps.

Robert loved UFOs. He thought they were vehicles for, or expressions of, so-called beings of light or angels or whatever people liked to call these entities. People who have experienced contact with these beings often report that they talk gibberish about existence, time and purpose – exactly the type of stuff that philosophers/deep thinkers talk nonsense about every day, to be fair. Robert wondered: *is it really all gibberish or is it a message from cosmic central that we can't grasp?* Yeah.

It was at that very moment that Robert himself started talking. He couldn't stop himself.

He was leaning on the window sill, looking so intently at the UFO as it inched and crawled across the sky, and what he said was like something that was unfolding unedited in his mind, a big imaginative unfiltered, unarranged sweep of language unfixed in context – in other words, Robert started talking complete and utter gibberish.

'Where am I? Like a million miles away and a million light years more. Where the dear roam. I want to take another drink and then drink some more. Where the fuck is this going? Down, down to the underground. But what's the command? Between science-dogma and sado-politico-religious hegemony, there's nowhere to run, never mind hide. Except here.

'Trying to avoid a big world sweep. It's not just money – it is your soul; all time control. *That* is the real energy which makes this mother ship work, it's all in the mind, right? Talk about a void before and behind. Mama, we're mental now. Cutting across and beyond righteous ritual , conditioning or even fear. The neural sensitive imprint in the brain is an addictive. It leaves you wanting more and more and more. More soul food, more sold food, more satisfaction. And the direction: express elevator up – to nothing. To the scaffold. But no direction at all because there is no reason to find anything, especially yourself. Because you wake up

'Feeling like someone different every day. An automatic writing for the big programme. What is more, the holy sacrament is, like DNA, inconclusive. Behind and before, no future in the universe's dreaming. A loaded grease gun stuck up time's ass. Out into space – the space and pattern between worlds where there's no big barrier, only pretty funny ugly shapes, stretching out, feeling and ticking. A little bit of automatic bonus – some more satisfaction. But it's all pseudonometry. A foamy war; the creation of a wave – silver like gold, except this serpent shines without glittering. Year in year out and in again. That is the rhythm; relentless like an old pig iron auto-hammer smashing down into thin invisible air for a millennium or two. Nothing but the hammer. No friction, no burn for anyone, behind and before. Free for all. Except for the world's forgotten boy. A street walking cheater. Intravenous Venus on a half shelf life. Why did I reject it? There must be six hundred and sixty six reasons. What the fuck, it didn't take in my head. And I was left to circumnavigate the orb, lots, lost and lonely. Looking for a kiss and a fix. Well, I'll fix it in the mix. Always. Cause I was the only one who had a reason for reason and the will to go about it. Yes, I had the smarts. A calling.

'And for money I will sell holy artefacts – a tea towel on which Elvis, an old time saint, is naked in all his glory, holding just his guitar, or an Elvis bedside clock where he winks, belches and slurs the words to his hymn *Old Shep* as you wake up.

'Yes, I was looking right into the eye of a tuneless moon when something fucking strange happened. A sister went weird on me – a freeze blank look in her eye, above and beyond the usual. Like she was possessed, not herself, although she and everyone else never is or are. She was spitting the most unusual little sayings which I was quick enough to write down. Man, the stuff – 'I am the axle of the wheel and the cube is the circle' and 'listen to the numbers and the words: 4 6 3 8 A B K 2 4 A L' and so forth and so on until there was enough mystery and history to fill a medium sized tome of 77 pages. Well I was a dog agog and when she finished she just sat and blinked and looked. She was the same and not. Only I could tell the difference. It was in her engine. Her brain. I knew that she was no longer on automatic. I was scared. One thing's as certain as the diamond glint crease in Elvis' pink peg slax, that big jumble of words was a revelation. A key. A weapon. And I was sure that the message was in the medium, the psychic. It was in the rhythm, a preternaturally constructed code to switch on or off, depending on how you look at it. So this was the reason why I was the world's forgotten boy. And now I knew, I blew. As far as I was concerned, this scene was as anti-life as a tube of lube on the extra quick. Utopia could wait! I could just about live on napalm dust economy. But then Crazy Time took a turn again. One hot evening, she spun brightly with only the fear light to guide her, telling things as they should or shouldn't be. I think my Holy Guardian Angel was talking. Strung out on lasers and climbing the chimney stacks along 22 paths that lead to right here and now.

'The angels flew, still gold but tarnished. Ready to storm the gates of heaven itself. As if I would! And now my Holy Guardian Angel informed me it was time to dry and fly and die, or all three. No time to adieu the vision or the voice. An erupting puzzle of periodical and cyclical amazement. I was Angel food. And it must have been something I ate. I woke up.

'The room was full of napalm smoke. It floated vertically like a wrong side wire. There windows but there were bars of flame across them. Which was bad. I think I had seen the room in my dreams before. The napalm smoke irritated my throat. So I called out: 'Fire!'

The door opened and a man jumped in. there were wings where his arms should be. He looked around, and asked: 'Where?' 'Down below,' I answered. He laughed. 'Where am I?' I asked. 'Exactly where you should be,' he said. 'We all are.' This made sense, at last. It was all adding up. He went out. The door shut. The place I am speaking about is in 22 places, and none of them are called 'home'.

'So that was the real nature of things. It was just business. You don't have to be clinical or cynical about it. You can spend your life fighting it, but your finger's always on the fast forward of desire and disaster. So here I am watching a heap of naked bodies falling through infinite space. Coiled heretic visions. Supra- Beatnik dreams – we are all Lucifer, aren't we? Jerking at the flailing of useless limbs and tensely contorted musculature as the disempowered drop sheer down into the void.

'Huh, I prefer 1960s chrome – all Sputnik red. Spunking up the night sky with voluptuous bearings – due east bright, sad star. But at the end I knew I would say: 'I was cured.' And this time I would mean it. Although there is no escape – instead a chiasmus – hell within me, within me: hell. Divine rhetoric. Like I was some Icarus, Prometheus, Faustus, Johnny Thunders – or any of those people like Lesley Winer who says: 'Words I have none, I just steal them to make them talk. I know they're stolen but I don't give a fuck.' I don't either.

'I just need a drink. Why does everything have to be so extreme? Why are they feeding me this dim star in isolation with nerve endings feedback-black like chrome that had been singed in a car wreck. Then maybe madness is what is all comes down to. The reason for all the ritual and the rightness, evocation with the aid of Evo-Stickschtick, gluing and pounding together all the crazy parts that add up to the hole. Where live all the Gods and dogs with their faceless faces and un-nameable name calling. Here at last I can reclaim my own freaky daemon. Like a falling star. Like paradise lost. That's where I am.'

Robert stopped talking. Then a long pause.

'Is that a beatnik thing? A beat poem?' Marlene asked – she'd hardly been listening, but she caught a few phrases. 'I think I can nick some of that for a song or a T-shirt or something.'

The UFO finally disappeared out of Robert's (and Marlene's) sight line.
Robert then said: 'What the fuck was that?'

He looked around, at Marlene and the small room, decorated with his *Anarchy in the UK* poster, and a picture of Patti Smith, and added, 'What the fuck is *this*?'

Gives you a real lift. For closer harmony.

✕

CHAPTER FOURTEEN

Nothing fits and everything seems imminent

Back inside the Camden flat Robert and Marlene were safe but still unsound – a fresh and strong wave of acid swept over them, sending the couple reeling into the bedroom.

The voices started chattering hard in Marlene's head. *Yadda yadda yadda.* On and on. If you've got nothing nice to say, say nothing – that's what Marlene's dead dad always said – so she didn't speak to him for a year. Now, she repeated the saying to him: *if you've got nothing nice to say, then shut your fucking big ugly mouth, dad.* But he would not be silent.

So, Marlene was almost glad when Robert started to unbutton her original Sex shirt, from the Kings Rd shop – if you're going to call a shop Sex and put the name up in big pink rubber letters it's pretty clear that you're really more interested in making a statement than in sex, it has been said – and this was echoed by many of those who wore the clothes, including and especially Marlene. She hated sex, but made Sex and Seditionaries clothes her *raison d'etre. Johnny Rotten wore a fucking bondage suit.* It was a religious experience. Marlene had bought the clothes up like they were going out of fashion, which they were – in the late 70s and very early 80s, when punk had finished and no one wanted the clothes anymore, you could buy them on the cheap. Marlene would wear the clothes until she could no longer fit in them – whereupon she would store them in a suitcase for ever and ever. Hidden, like her.

Robert thought, craft must have clothes but truth loves to go naked, which was the slogan graffitied behind that big pink Sex sign, and continued to strip Marlene. She was glad because even though she hated Robert and his stupid thick cock, sex might distract her from what the voices in her head were saying – *fucking shit cunts.*

'Let's lie down,' said Robert. By which he meant 'Let's fuck,' of course.

Marlene could hear his cock harden. It sounded... hairy. 'Ooh, that acid,' she gasped.

Any stimulant, no matter how weak – he had to be careful with strongly brewed tea – made Robert want to have sex. With the acid pulsing through him, his lust was off the scale. He hurried and fumbled with various buttons, zips and straps – fucking bondage trousers – the strap was always getting in the way when you least need it to – running away from Teds and other idiots in the past, fumbling in bed these days.

Marlene, meanwhile, lay back and allowed herself to be undressed completely. She had to admit, the acid was giving her a little tingle, too. The nakedness, the openness, the saliva, the mess – it usually made her sick, but the acid made it almost bearable.

She looked at Robert – saliva was falling from his mouth in anticipation, it seemed to her. Streams and globs of it hanging from his open, leering mouth. The dirty fucker, she thought.

Robert took his own clothes off quickly. Marlene looked at him. Black hair. Sometimes it was red, or another colour, sometimes it was blonde – but not for ages – she was glad because that would have clashed with Colin. Two blondes – too much! She insisted that Robert dye his hair black. *Now, they were salt and pepper.* If she had ever been into having a threesome with the two of them, which she never was, *God fucking forbid, one at a time is too much,* it would at least have looked aesthetically balanced. But, Robert's hair looked longer, she hated long hair – fucking hippie.

She looked more closely at him, and recoiled. Not only was his hair too long, it looked like it had spread down his chest and back and, well, every fucking where. Robert had a pelt! His build was more powerful now, had he been down the gym? His forehead was wide, *Jesus his jaw looked strong,* his nose was blunt. *Christ.* She rubbed her eyes. His ears were relatively small and triangular and the limbs long and robust, with comparatively small... paws! *Robert has turned into an animal. He had turned into a fucking full-on wolf!*

And did that make her Little Red Riding hood? Of course it did.

Robert sighed a little – but to Marlene it sounded like a series of growls, barks, and whines. *As long as he didn't start fucking howling – let's think of the neighbours here.*

Robert wanted her from behind, on her knees. Of course he did. He tapped her flank. Marlene liked to fuck in the dark, but some light shone in through the blinds from the lamppost outside – the shadows fell on their bodies, stripes of human experience, savage yet delicately rhapsodic.

She turned over and he mounted her, covered her, and tried to put his cock in. Now, Marlene knew little about wolves or their anatomy – but she seemed to remember there was a penis hook involved that acted like nature's Velcro – locking the male and female together until the male's sperm had had a chance to impregnate his mate before any rival could try his luck. And Colin wasn't even here! In any case, the whole thing made her feel a little nervous. So, Robert had a little trouble inserting himself, but putting his hand on the base of her back, he slowly managed it.

She gasped. She didn't like sex with humans never mind wolves – but novelty of it did something to her, she had to admit. And of course she knew it wasn't *a real fucking wolf, don't be fucking stupid – but then what the fuck was real anyway*? She had no idea anymore.

Robert took her roughly. Of course he did. The company of wolves, so it goes.

Animals never seem to enjoy sex. Marlene thought. She'd only seen pigeons shagging, and dogs of course, but she had the impression that the female just wanted it to finish as soon as it started – which, on an everyday basis, was just like her. So, yes, she agreed with herself, in that respect *you could call me an animal. You hear that dad, Branco, all you other fuckers and fuckwits – you've been calling me that for years and I agree, I'm a fucking animal.* She sang to herself: *She was a no-one who killed her baby/She sent her letters from the country/She was an animal/She was a bloody disgrace – and don't give me those looks,* she said to the dead babies. The dead babies were staring at her. The dead babies were watching. Which, since one of the dead babies belonged to Robert, made this... a Primal Scene.

Pigs. She'd also seen pigs having a go at each other once. Quite a production. But she didn't like to think of pigs. She saw herself as quite pig like. And it wasn't a nice feeling. Pigs are quite ugly. *Ugly.* She almost dried up at the thought of it. *Ug face. Frog face.* Branco had left her for a girl with classic good looks. *I will castrate him, and will gut her. Frog face. That's what they used to call me.* But her dad said she was beautiful... inside. *I've got a face that will get better with age – I will grow into it. It will look better when I'm older.* She thought.

The world will love me. The fucking world – I will spit in its fucking eye. The world huffed and it puffed and tried to blow me the fuck down.

She squealed out loud. Robert thought it just the acid squealing. He didn't let it put him off his stroke. It was hard to distract him once he'd got going.

I'm a pig with a frog's face, groaned Marlene. Sometimes Robert liked to fuck in front of the mirror – *but there's no way I'm looking in any fucking mirrors on acid,* thought Marlene. Imagine! *But I'm beautiful person inside. My dad told me. The fucking great liar. Aren't you, dad? You cunt with your fucking cancer. He. Them. Boys. They tried to blow me down, and yes I blew some of them. But not my dad! They tried to tear me down. They tried to tear me. The big fucking bad wolf.*

She was glad that Robert was taking her from behind – she didn't want to look in his eyes. She didn't want to see a reflection of herself in his eyes. And she didn't want to share the wild feelings that had doubtless set his eyes alight.

'Do you want me to eat you?' whispered Robert in Marlene's ear.

'Nooo!' cried Marlene...

'OK, I was just asking,' said Robert, a little confused. Marlene never usually turned down the offer of oral sex.

Marlene looked back over her shoulder at him. She looked at his mouth. *Never realised how big it was. Wide. Sensuous. Enticing smile. But those teeth! My God how sharp they look.*

Marlene went into an acid reverie. A gothic fever dream.

'What a big mouth you have,' she said in a trembling voice to the wolf.

'All the better to eat you with!' growled the wolf, dressed in her mum's clothes, *no not my mum's!* – anyway, it was a strange looking wolf, it had a tail like a fox's and ears pricked like a dog's. *Probably symbolic,* she thought, *now I'm really in trouble.*

The wolf jumped out of bed, and ate her up in one lick, swallowing her whole. Then the beast, with a stomach full, sated, fell asleep, snoring – *like all these fuckers do after they've had what they wanted,* she thought. Marlene curled up in a foetal ball in the wolf's stomach, closed her eyes and dreamt. A dream within a dream.

A hunter who, weirdly, looked like a wolf himself, had appeared from the dark forest. He saw the wolf with the fat bulging stomach, as if pregnant.

'The wolf! He won't get away this time!' said the hunter.

And without further ado, he cut open the wolf's stomach. 'You'll never bother anyone ever again,' he said, shaking a fist that looked like a paw.

And to his utter amazement, from the wolf's stomach out popped Branco, Marlene's dad, Robert, a few dead kids, and some other horrible people, all saying really *ugly* things. Last but not least came Marlene herself.

She had been saved.

'Next time, keep to the path,' said the hunter who took Marlene – her hand in his paw and led her away...

'No!' cried Marlene in panic.

'OK, fine, I heard you, I won't go down on you!' said Robert, 'I wasn't suggesting anal sex or anything. Christ!'

The wolf and the ass – there is a fable in there somewhere, a ludicrous fairy tale. One with a moral.

'Do you know the Aesop fable?' he asked her. 'The wolf and the ass.'

Marlene didn't. But pondered. Perhaps Robert wasn't the wolf, perhaps he was the ass in wolf's clothing?

Just as she was beginning to come around to the idea that maybe Robert only looked like a wolf, he bent down and bit her on the spot where neck and shoulder meet. Hard.

While Robert had been steadily fucking Marlene, he had increasingly come to realise that something was wrong. He fucked her this way. He fucked her that way. He stroked her breasts. He sniffed her belly button. He sniffed her arse. She just didn't feel or smell like herself – sour and bitter. Now she smelt: mass-produced. With a chemical tang that scrambled Robert's senses a little more, if that was possible. And she felt to the touch: fabricated. He stroked her hair

– how stiff it was. Like a wig. Her pubes, too. They were obviously man made. That was it. Marlene was made of plastic! But was she some kind of life-sized plastic model? Or, was she a blow up doll? He suspected the latter – the innermost her behind the veil.

He hated the thought that he was fucking a blow up doll. He once knew a guy who knew a guy who worked in a Soho sex shop. The guy sold a doll to a Chinese chap. Later that day, the man came back to return the doll – deflated, stuffed crudely back in the box, obviously used. What was wrong with it? 'Ah so!' said the man. The Soho guy said: 'Sorry?' The man pointed to the crotch. 'No, ah so.' 'Ah so?' 'Yes, ah so!' 'Oh.' It clicked, the plastic sex doll was not equipped with an anus. Crushed, the backdoor man had brought it back. Robert laughed when he heard the story – but understood where the guy was coming from – or not as the case may be.

Still the idea of fucking a blow up doll didn't amuse him – he didn't want to be like the Soho tossers. He was better than that. There was only one way to find out the truth about this doll business... he bent down as if to kiss Marlene, bared his teeth and bit.

'Argh,' shouted Marlene, muting herself quickly after remembering their neighbours. 'What the fuck do you think you're doing?' she stage whispered.

Well, she didn't burst or quickly deflate, but Robert still wasn't completely sure whether or not she was a blow up doll. Every picture of a blow-up doll he'd seen had been as ugly as sin, with an asymmetric body. The Soho sex shop guy had remarked, 'Never mind about the lack of arse, who would want to fuck someone who looks like a frog princess with Downs Syndrome?' Not a nice thing to say. Robert resolved not to repeat that to Marlene. He asked her straight: 'Look, are you a blow up doll or not, Marlene?'

'What?' She exclaimed. 'I'll fucking blow you up. You stupid cunt.' She wanted to lash out but restrained herself.

Robert turned Marlene onto her back, raised her legs over his shoulders and, realising his time in Marlene was perhaps approaching an end, took her hard and fast.

He looked at her naked left foot by his face. Robert didn't really like Marlene's feet – they were too claw- like, lacking sensuality. But sometimes a naked foot is a naked foot – and that is enough. He started to come.

He looked down and saw that his penis was no longer engorged flesh, pulsing with sperm, but a fountain – a large ornate fountain in a sunny city – one that gushed water from its spout – a steady surge that continued for hours, days, aeons – like time lapse filming – with those sped-up clouds flying across the screen – and finally, after eternity, after generations had been born, had lived, gone about their lives as best they could, and died – finally, the water from the baroque fountain stopped. The world was left to lament that the beautiful fountain had dried up. The fountain fed by, and feeding all of the rivers, lakes, seas and oceans in the world had emptied itself, and the world felt regret.

Robert pulled his cock out, a last drop of liquid fell on Marlene's pubes. He flopped on the bed exhausted. Marlene dug him in the ribs with her fist.

'Oof,' he said.

'Ah so,' said Marlene.

'What?'

'Arsehole. Have you ever seen your own arsehole?' she asked him.

This was obviously a philosophical riddle, one that Robert would ponder over for years to come.

Looking for a Kiss

✕

CHAPTER FIFTEEN

Get the picture?

One day, Marlene came back from somewhere, and flopped down on the bed. She didn't say where she'd been, but Robert presumed she'd been with Colin, taking drugs and having some sort of sex.

Robert thought the scene before him, Marlene face down on the bed, silver/white cropped hair, the light pouring in and out via the window above the bed, skirt pulled down slightly at the back, half exposing large silver/white buttocks, bare feet, looked like a tainted pop statement, either a warm up or aftermath to a porn shoot, a murder scene, an anti-glamour crisis, or a sensitive meditation on form and (what's the) matter. All of that.

He snapped the scene two or three times on his Kodak instant. The pictures developed in front of his very eyes. Magic.

In the future, Robert mused on whether or not one of these photos would work as a cover for a book – the one describing this story.

His friend Boogie said the pictures were too much like Nan Goldin's.

Robert loved Goldin. He'd recently seen her *Memory Lost* exhibition in London. He wrote about it for an arts journal.

'Although *Memory Lost*, the centre piece of *Sirens*, Nan Goldin's first solo exhibition for 12 years looks backwards, comprising old work both previously seen and unseen, it's far from being a simple retrospective – and it's clear why Goldin herself considers it to be a major fresh work.

'*Memory Lost* is a 45-minute slideshow of pictures, music and dialogue, the main theme of which is addiction.

'The slideshow format – *a la* her ground breaking work *The Ballad of Sexual Dependency* – is perfect for Goldin's oeuvre. Images pulse and disappear: a flickering zoetrope of pictures – almost ephemeral – like a drug rush, a hit; easy come easy go easy come again.

'We see:-

'... Cookie Mueller, smouldering with a certain confused impatience... drugs... Religious icons (kitsch – the chosen iconography style of melodrama and excess), milk/water flowing from a statuette's breasts...

'It's also a fast flow of feelings; as if to maintain that it isn't actually true that life isn't worth living unless you pause now and then to reflect that you are alive.

'... a drooping, withered Xmas tree ... messy hotel rooms... wrecked rooms... disturbing self-portraits (a molten/bemused quality in her eyes, as though she had seen or imagined bad sad things – especially in the mirror, perhaps)...

'The show is carried by the type of rhythm that opens up the borders of slippery psychological complexity.

'... New York City... the projects... a horrific slit wrist... drugs... a drug neighbourhood... a shitty mattress ruined by a large 'fall-unconscious-with-a-cigarette' hole burnt all the way through, springs and wires exposed like nerves...

'Art and fame, sex and money all blurred together like wild forces we can't control.

'... pills in an open safe ...

'It's a revelation, almost traumatic – art that feels like a physical sensation. Emotions drift like the swirls in a drug user's spoon.

'The visuals are underpinned by a haunting, doleful new score by composer Mica Levi, which takes the dread to the next level. The dialogue, comprising phone messages and snippets of conversations, overlays the music and the pictures with musings and utterances benumbed – from or about people who, at some point, have lost the thread of the track of their own lives:-

'... coke or dope... wake up...wake up...wake up... wake up... in mom's arms, that's where I felt safe and secure... I would put 'dead' by people's names but then there were so many I gave up... are you OK? Call me. Are you eating? What's happening? ... I couldn't leave the house – the beautiful leaves turning making me ... it must be the fall ... the fall... just trying not to feel anything... you don't ever belong... took the money and keys and left me in the room for five days – I couldn't get drugs and it was like being buried alive... he doesn't know how to cry anymore – just makes noises... connection – that's what people are looking for in addiction...

'Goldin came to prominence by presenting, with bravery, empathy and downbeat pizzazz, the 'holy moment' of photography, when the camera's gaze alights on the real, however provocative it may be: fixed, unspeakable reality. Fixed and unspeakable perhaps because, as writer Ann Marlowe says, addiction – and it was always there in the background – stops time – physically, emotionally, philosophically – it is 'a form of mourning for irrecoverable glories'. In other words, nostalgia in its most alarming form – one which 'stops your passage to the future'.

'In this respect, *Memory Lost* is anything but nostalgic. Instead – and this is the point – it reframes, recasts, recalibrates the past in order to present an arc. That of the subjects who embody *Memory Lost*'s theme – it recognises that head, heart and psyche of the drug user is either filled with light or horror, depending on the point travelled on the spiral. And that of the artist herself – asserting that memory is not a fixed concept and that we can and do recontextualize to make sense of a given narrative – and it's this that offers nothing less and nothing more than a sense of fresh possibility.'

Robert thought: I know this life, I know this art, I am glad that Goldin has found redemption.

He decided not to put one of the Kodak instant photos on the cover of the book. *Maybe elsewhere, in a different context.* He thought. Context is everything. *Nan knows this better than anyone.*

✕

CHAPTER SIXTEEN

A compelling tale

Some hours later. The sun had come up, spreading warmth. Robert and Marlene were on the bed, freezing. But still naked. The acid had worn off to a large degree. They had both had enough.

Robert was no longer able to look into the future at will. The visions of unfolding events that he had seen and felt, would not be remembered. Sometimes, over the years, he would get the feeling that something very valuable had been in his embrace, his possession. But he could not remember exactly what. It was like a dream that he would forever try to recall. Also, he knew, even though it was a platitude – *people forever veer from platitudes to dramatics and back*, he thought – that the only way to tell the future was to make it. Truly make it.

The voices in Marlene's head had stopped for the time being.

Robert could see the defining black lines of the colouring book very clearly once more.

'Bloop!' he said very softly as an understated finale, for old time's sake.

But the wild hallucinations had been replaced by the sense that they were both looking at the world through a slightly dirty Perspex screen. There was a barrier between themselves and what they saw. It was almost ironic – the revenge of the Gods – that they, who had always held the normal world in contempt, were now removed from it – they both wrung their hands in consternation and agony. One definition of hell is simply separation from God, so Robert and Marlene's Hell was separation from the normal world. They could not touch it, or feel it – it was as though they had both been put in a small cell from which they could vaguely view the outside, but not take part in it on any level. Two damned souls writhing. They desperately wanted nothing more than for everything to be as it always had been. Instead, their feelings had been bleached out, and it had been this way for a while. Robert, who was interested in the idea of 'distance', 'remoteness' and cool, was now trapped tightly in a vast cold space.

For how long, he wondered?

Marlene started to cry. She would have sobbed her
heart out, *if she had one*, joked Robert to himself.

'It's going to be like this forever, isn't it?' she said, panicking. 'We're like those casualties you hear about – the ones who've gone out too far and can never come back.'

Robert said nothing. And he didn't hold Marlene to comfort her.

'Next time, let's just take speed,' she said. 'If there is a next time. If I'm not in a loony bin. I can't take this anymore. I want to come back.'

Robert took his mind off the situation by working out how this part of story could be written up, or filmed, maybe. He envisaged a loop of the scene broken down into different parts – but the dialogue accompanying each part would change at random – so it would never ever be the same. Out of sync, too, Robert added as an afterthought. Perfect dislocation.

'We just have to let the acid wear off completely, don't worry,' he said. But he was a little concerned himself – he'd never know the tail end of a trip, with its very real sense of dissociation to last for so long. Perhaps they *would* be eternal drug victims. But, no, that would be crazy, it would be punishment outweighing the crime – an injustice – and he was a person who believed in natural justice. Justice just is, as it were.

He said: 'We just have to wait.' Marlene continued to cry.

He repeated: 'Just wait.'

And so they waited. Naked and afraid.

Marlene waited: -

... to say to herself: I have been dispossessed of my identity, *I* have dispossessed myself of my identity.

... for all the pity in this world and the next.

... to recognise the qualities and benefits of anxiety.

... for someone who would reveal herself to herself.

... for the ghost of her father to tell a joke. A good one.

... for the age of confession and spurious grievance.

... to paint a stupid and disturbing self-portrait.

... to stop the future and the past *and fucking let me off.*

... for anything but nostalgia.

... to make the mistake of putting knowledge above imagination.

... to assume the eternal values of the supermarket.

Robert waited:-

... to get paid for daydreaming.

... to richly possess a number of 'poor objects.'

... for a sign directing him to the last remote Badlands.

... to sit quietly in a room.

... to go uptown and downtown.

... for writing – his own, that is – which feels like a physical sensation.

... to realise that words are never enough.

... for 'soul food and a place to eat'.

They both waited:-

... for the taste of decay/death in their mouths to diminish. (Robert: *Corpse in my mouth? I'm a fucking vegan!*)

... to understand the real meaning of the phrase: the politics of boredom.

... to laugh *with* not *at* Kafka: 'There is hope – but not for *us*.'

... Zen silence.

... to become familiar characters to themselves.

... to disappear here, and there.

Put some romance in your life. Another dream satisfied.

×

POSTSCRIPT

Diary Entries 1988-89

Tuesday April 19 1988

Reviewing Frank Zappa at the Wembley Arena. Meet Terry. Drinks in Soho, drinks in Wembley, drinks at the party afterwards, drinks at Terry's till 6am: I slid into oblivion to wake up in a Hackney hell hole, fully clothed with a duvet thrown over me. XXXX and XXXX arrive with three dogs – one of them very licky. I resign myself to wasting another day through alcohol. Not only waste but suffer – my come downs are enormous; depression – I feel like weeping uncontrollably, mainly cause I have to work and all I want to do is curl up with a book. But I must be Jeffrey Bernard about it – a guy who was sacked many times for drunkenness beyond the call of duty.

Saturday April 23 1988

I am a disgrace to the human race...

Wednesday April 27 1988

... illness seeping through me but I don't realise it till I awake after a night of being physically crushed and hung upside down in a little ball and twisted around by a huge pair of hands like a malleable piece of green snot... experiences and joy = progress of soul but ditto the shit of nothing in private and personal hell of sterility – where is the fame and respect owed to a serious artist of the wastelands who isn't a real artist?

Wednesday May 4 1988

In West End, meet a crazed XXXX in tune with debauch and insanity. Drunk, she says she fucked XXXX, 'he was good' – I don't care. But she might regret it. Off to Camberwell where I fuck her on all fours. I put a finger up her ass, a shiny tube. She wiped the spunk from between her legs with my clean Seditionaries T shirt. Apt. I should get a wardrobe or rack – all those clothes I hang in the windows and around the room are fucked by the sun... then I went up to XXXX's to watch a bit of the '66-'68 series on TV – Situationists and Co twenty years on – all the rebels are fatter and balder – just like the punks now – with nothing gained but regression, perhaps. Two ex-lovers talk about their time together, their betrayals. They seem empty and resigned to emptiness. *C'est la vie.* Not for me. We'll see. Keep going and hope for a break – yeah, break my heart.

Friday May 20 1988

Hung around some of the seedier Soho dives – including the Dive Bar in China Town, where I chatted to a cute girl – she didn't like Ray, who seemed to frighten the girls – he's socially inept, intense and shy, but come on, he's not frightening – before being dragged off to the Intrepid Fox, where I got distracted by blonde from Birmingham – kissed and then... later made my excuses and went up to XXXX's to watch *Letters from a Dead Man* – a Russian treatment of a post-nuclear holocaust situation. Romantic and philosophical. Poetic certainly. The West could never come up with something like this. I'm almost proud to originate in blood from this vague part of the world... I read the *NME* and discover they've printed hate letters directed towards me from Zappa fans about my review. Can't even remember writing it... listen to a pirate reggae show on the radio – it keeps me going.

Wednesday May 25 1988

XXXX rang me to say she missed me (!?), I was supposed to meet her but let's bear in mind... the Patrick Walker horoscope warns me that the relationship set up will have to be examined. I know... and money is a worry.

Thursday 26 May to Monday 30 May 1988

Have wasted the past few days drunk – to keep from screaming with/ from fear/boredom – in the pool rooms of Camden with the Americans. And then had wallet stolen in Covent Garden when I was too busy smiling incoherently and dragging my misspent youth into a misspent life. Later, we – the lost ones – staggered off – Terry, Gerard, Mick (and Margaret) (she is in brackets because she is not quite as lost as the rest of us?) to more pool rooms with GBH north Londoners with time done and time to lose.

Up next day and went on a wild frightening car ride with Terry to sign on as a failure in Peckham dole office. Look forward to £66 from Thursday. Please. Bow wow.

We play chess. 'You're playing like a master,' says Terry. But I can't keep it up. He says: 'You are Crowley the chess master!' Ha. But without the artistic anti-logic. Just the haphazard little flashes of joy while moving those pieces, like I'm creating situations (good practice for).

I read Donleavy's *A Fairy Tale of New York* where Christian, across the Atlantic, struggles to find something that fits in the craziness before going mad surrounded by women and money and death – and there he is, so polite, longing for the composure of the English for God's sakes. Without question marks, as if to say what's the point in asking (*you get no reply*). I can relate to this book

Thursday June 2 1988

These days everyone sees life as a big mind game and a battle. Everyone getting one up on everyone else. I heard someone say: 'The good thing about being out of it and being in an argument is the thought: if I were straight I'd slaughter this guy.' What a wanker. The nasty side has really come out in people nowadays. People act like little kids all the time everywhere. If you take people and society seriously – that's the way to lose track and hope... bad phone call from XXXX – picking at each other and I slammed the phone down... this part of the journal was actually written sitting at my desk instead of lying on the bed – an attempt to become a real writer. Real writers sit at desks.

Thursday June 23 1988

Missed out on reviewing the Big Audio Dynamite LP, and have had enough of the *NME*. It's rubbish and people like XXXX are part of the forces of conservatism, really. Should have gone to see Strummer at the Fridge, but it would have been yet another drunken whirl. I'm not in the mood. Although the prospect of seeing XXXX is enticing. To fuck her little arse and make her squeal – like Saturday, sucking her cunt avidly, which may have produced moans, I don't know. I put it in her. She came – it always amazes me when I make someone come. To end off the romance I called her a beautiful girl and she called me a beautiful boy. Then I had a piss.

Monday June 27 1988
A disturbing dream. I and a group of people/friends are in the garden of a house – Dunstable? – a tower dominates the immediate skyline. As if it were on top of the Dunstable Downs and the Downs were my garden. The tower leans, begins to fall. Tottering on the edge. Dilapidated. It's inevitable. In slow motion almost. We run back into the house. In apparent security we listen to chunks of it falling all around. I remember no more – *I am under the tower that falls!*

Wednesday July 6 1988
The 'squat' / housing association place in Camberwell may be a run-down tip, but at least I have the mental free space to forge some sort of future for myself... meet XXXX to talk convulsively about desperation (mine), future (hers) and Gorbachov – the beer spins in us and we fall in bed – I can't even remember how we fucked except just shoving it into her and then wetting XXXX's fingers with my spit and placing them on her clit until she whimpered for mercy so I stopped and fell asleep. This was the beginning of my downfall – my thoughts next day were scattered and work left unfinished – time is running out and I'm running after it.

Thursday July 7 July 1988
A sauna and steam – with ice cold plunge pool! – in Brixton leisure centre. Feel better. Fix XXXX's curtain rail – better than going out getting drunk.

Tuesday July 12 1988
Do I have a destiny or am I a slug? Am I a man or a slug slithering into oblivious obscurity leaving a shiny/dull trail that people, if they notice it, probably won't even wonder what happened to the slug that made it. I'm

in a limp-cock backwater, which I'm treading, head just above the surface.

Later, rehearsals with new band, Woman – creativity introduced into the order of the day – I extend myself on guitar – I *wanked* my broken down shit Shaftesbury guitar just like Patti Smith said – but I probably need a Strat. Talking of Patti, I meet Jane Suck at the *NME*. She tells me to fuck off. I tell her to fuck off. We fuck off.

Saturday July 30 1988
Recover from XXXX from King Kurt's party. Talked at length to thin, old Kings Road shop manager (at Smiths) – making cracks, getting slapped. Then she invited me to the Grove tomorrow (today). I'm not sure. I can't get drunk again. It just leads to vegetation. My 80s: Half vegetable half animal.

Monday August 1 1988
To the Scala to see *Ironweed* with cans of lager. Then the Swag Club, empty apart from some Swedish tourists – talked to one. Nice. Earlier, had successfully avoided some American woman in Bloomsbury. Later, chat to Virginia – the Saatchi & Saatchi cute girl – she'd been to the Pyramid Club. Wish I had, too.

Friday August 5 1988
Up very late and feel sick with myself for drinking. Dejected. Saved from myself by Jack who drags me off to guitar playing and... drinks. We chat over the usual emotions. Can't get inside this diary, or my own head. 'Love is a ghost'. Overwhelming sense of defeat, futility. XXXX's phone is dead which is lucky because I would have taken her out for a drink – and I would have felt bored and bad.

Monday August 8 1988
So the newspapers have pointed out, today is the eighth month of the eighty eighth (and a hundred) year. 8.8.88. In China they're going mental – the inauguration of their biggest building has been left till now, the maternity wards have been booked etc. In England no one

gives a shit. It's not a case of superstition, but one of care about the universe and one's position in it. The bottom line being, if you make a date important it will become important. And how have I spent this magical day? Wondering how to transform my existence, that is how. Deciding not to feel guilty about the past, to realise that my present position means fuck all, and that I need to (make a) move.

Tuesday August 9 1988

Barfly at the Scala. Mickey Rourke like he's playing WC Fields – is that how Bukowski talked? But it's shit – having no real story is permissible for a Bukowski movie, but no insight, no cut, no broken bottle from tracts of the dregs of humanity thrust into your face – no.

Dinner with Andrew Kotting – oddball king of Bohemia – honest, inquisitive, south London geezer, a bit thuglike – like a mad and perverse Jan Kramer. Interesting. I like him. We arrange to play football.

Saturday August 13 1988

In the sun up at Brockwell Park, but the lido wasn't open. At night, the Loughborough Junction hotel. XXXX chatted to me while I sat on the bar over her – she brushed my knees and smiled up. We fucked for three hours. I tied her legs and made her hold her arms above her head. Talked incessant obscenities into her ears. I spurted into her. She wanted me to suck her off. 'You expect me to put my tongue down there after I've just come?' I said. 'Just keep it above, on my clit,' she said. And I did... next day sun and sea in Sussex. Later Sussex in the dark – tree shapes with, surely, their spirits freaking about at the roadside. Revelling in the dusk. Weary travellers saved only by the roadside coffee inns. Preferable, the echoes of ritual and unbridled nature – wandering of villagers, mob, tribe and highwayman, to the violent modern suburbia... Education: Me: 'When will the world wake up to my talent?' XXXX: 'When will *you* wake up?'

Thursday August 25 1988

... my orgasm was impeded by an unrolled foreskin! I just stared into space...

Monday September 5 1988

I feel negative and depressed. Patrick Walker in the *Standard* says 'be more optimistic'. What does he know? It comes down to my desires and needs. Maybe I need security? Heavenly, bestial cuties are for youngsters, who cares about that when you get older? Maybe a woman with her own place and a yearning for kids and some unhurried weekends should be what I'm aiming for? In any event, it is time to move on. Where? To the wasteland? I am already here... XXXX comes round and we drink four pints in the Canning. She's a wild child. And she worries me. XXXX phones later. Pete Clag is dead. Died in his sleep from 'natural causes'. If being an alcoholic is natural that is. I looked out of the window and spooked myself out. Mortality touched us all that night. I won't make the funeral. I will write a letter of condolence to KW, whose review I did not write. Still, you can't please everyone.

Thursday 15 September 1988

Weird dream.

Danny Kelly from the *NME* starred in it as some sort of God. Sean O'Hagan and I visit him at his semi-penthouse flat to fawn. Someone says something about me looking like I've put on weight. I retaliate by pointing out Danny's humungous size. The situation is ugly. I'm not sure whether I get beaten up or not. But in any case I have to return to the flat later somehow to get Danny to clear things up and get me off the hook with his angry followers. In the maze-like building it's hard to find his room. Eventually one of his minions tells me the way. He's asleep laid out like a fat fuck emperor lying in state on a huge raised platform, difficult to wake. He's a cross between Colonel Kurtz in *Apocalypse Now* and the Godfather. He's groggy. I think he is maybe pleased that I've come to him for help. But I sense that what he wants, I am unable to give. It all looks grim for me!

Thursday October 20 1988

Interviewed XXXX XXXX in his Maida Vale flat. I ask if he ever gets lonely. He says, 'I suppose so. Everyone does. If you haven't got kids your life has to be your work. What else is there, just get pissed all the time?' Yeah, there has to be something more. I am becoming boring.

Friday October 21 to Wednesday 26 October 1988
Soundtrack: *Come Friday* – Wide Boy Awake.

Meet XXXX – good to see her after a week and a bit. She's looking beaten up by herpes and thin, but beautiful. Will someone take her away from me I wonder? Yeah, come Friday

See *Virgin* in the Rank preview theatre with K. She talks jealously about P's money, moans about how much she has. She is fixated. And a real tight wad. So much for her socialist cred. Film was great.

Monday October 31 1988
Halloween. The Union of Christian Teachers are applying pressure to have this pagan and evil festival banned. I don't care. I'm doing nothing to celebrate it. Selfish of me. This is a time to remember the dead and I should think of Danuta, and I do. But I feel something in the atmosphere. Apprehension, melancholy, fear. Or is it because I've spent three days curled up with XXXX (why was I going to say Danuta then?) and now I'm out on my own in the big wide world. On my own. People are out having fun. Some of us have to stay in and worry about the future.

Friday November 4 1988
Woken today by the sound of XXXX going psychotically crazy, swearing at XXXX, smashing the table with a ladder, of all things. What a nutcase! It was all about someone leaving the door on the latch. XXXX weeps profusely in her room. I'll comfort her later. Must get a place of my own.

Will I ever get Genesis P-Orridge interview sorted out? I bet he doesn't have to put up with this rubbish. Just invokes the evil spirits or something. Crass thing to say, I know.

Bike nicked after puncture on the way to New Cross.

A couple of phone calls from Tony D and XXXX have interrupted the flow this of this.

Saturday November 5 1988

Met Terry in the Cambridge. I drank blackcurrant juice – ah the joys of being teetotal for a night. He's off to Portugal. Split with XXXX again. Living like a tramp I just realised, but his vision is magical – 'From the walls/wars of Persia to the French Revolution there is an unbroken chain. A big wall around us. Leading to America, designed to get us to Sirius. The Russians fit in as being Mongolian. The Wicca people want to retain the earth.' I like it. He's mad, of course.

Monday November 14 1988

Why am I writing so strangely? So rhetorically? Loosen up! My speech has assumed a clipped, meaningful tone, but where has the zest and colour gone? ... rash on my arms. Vaguely worrying... XXXX's floundering about, looking for a future, just like everyone else. She has a panic stricken crying fit. Then we share a freaky boredom which we don't explore. But we hold hands... none of it is enough.

Sunday November 27 1988

Bile in my system. Wanted to be alone. Claustrophobia. But went to see old Anarchist films – the Situationists, cadre against cadre – hopeless. Cold Hackney. Cold.

Monday November 28 1988

Midnight. Soundtrack: Gospel Show on Studio FM.

Wednesday November 30 1988

Lethargy at XXXX's for a couple of days. Comfortable. Too comfortable. Coming out of it is like emerging from a strange, sleepy alternative world – and then I'm alone, depressed, active, frustrated, fighting – in other words... alive!

Tuesday January 3 1989

I need new beginnings. Much energy begat only by energy. Love begat only by love. A persistent effort in my affairs. And honesty in my dealings and conversations with people. And a new bike.

Tarot for the New Year.

Situation – Queen of Wands/ Seven of Wands/Four of Wands

Future One – Ace of Cups/FOOL/Eight of Pentacles

Future Two – Three of Wands/EMPEROR/STAR Psychological basis – Two of Pentacles/Knight of Pentacles/Four of Pentacles.

Karma – FORTUNE/DEATH/10 of Swords

Situation – Energy at last gasp, obstacles but must get courage to meet them, persistent energy needed. Future One – Fertility, ideas, new era, new error

Future Two – Success after struggle, power, hope and clarity.

Psychological basis – harmony and dullness

Karma – Change of fortune, sudden and unexpected change, disruption.

Tuesday January 24 1989

Went round to Tom's to get a copy of *Vague*. He's been watching IRA funeral videos for his birthday treat. Man, he needs cheering up. Same goes for a lot of people, I suppose.

XXXX has been ill for ages. Suspicion about a contagious chest infection. And now I'm feeling pretty awful – psychological? – long hot soak hasn't helped that much.

Wednesday January 25 1989

But, God (why am I talking to God? Why not?), I should be exploring ways of beating reality and not just escaping it, as they say. But I'm just avoiding it for the time being. I'm interviewing the Shamen. Jeez, what do I care about these people? Nothing... XXXX is *always* ill. Maybe I should get her something for the weekend – like... a doctor. Let's pray she hasn't got AIDS, or I've got it, too. How selfish? Bought a mountain bike, £125 plus £16.50p lock – I will save £34 in Capital Cards for the next month.

Friday January 27 1989

Cheese sandwich, mushroom noodle soup, a can of crucial brew, a bottle of Pils, two or three bags of crisps, fags.

Monday February 13 1989

Rolled around Soho with Terry and then did it all over again next night at the Johnny Thunders gig. Terry had a drug dealer smashing up his room and fucking his ex. Who needs it? How come my journal is just full of moans and hopes and not the in-depth look at art and humanity that it should be?

Tuesday February 14 1989

Tom Vague rings about trip to Paris, to the Situationist event. Savage and Jamie Reid are going, too. I don't have the time or money.

£16 for a new driving test, £11 for calor gas, £47 fine for tax (not paid). Borrowed £60 off XXXX .

Fucked XXXX. She put a Johnny on me. After she came I couldn't get the tension going. Even thinking of XXXX couldn't get me flowing. Took XXXX from behind, ludicrously banged my head on the low ceiling – that stupid platform bed is bad news for doggie style. Good title for a book?

Friday February 17 1989

Lonely. But then at the Grove met XXXX – God knows why I ever had a thing with her. Her mate XXXX is a real human and a laugh. Told her she'd look great with a pair of knuckledusters on. Good chat up line!

Monday February 20 1989

Reading *Wonderland Avenue* by Danny Sugerman for the interview – heroin and cocaine, the Whiskey, Rainbow Rooms, Sunset Boulevard, collapse, hospital, psychiatrist. The moral of the story: be rich or have a rich father. But the real moral of the story: stop fucking about and get down to write and... write! XXXX gone to LA (to meet Danny Sugerman?) I've got to find something. I need something.

Sunday March 5 1989

I'm short of breath and short of friends. Fucked XXXX in the morning, and she put a Johnny on me again (what's going on?) – but the phone rang , and it rang for ages and ages and it put me off. I couldn't help thinking it was bad news, Or good. It gets to be the same thing in a way. And then I thought of maybe get some speed, maybe pay my tax, about how I hate that guy who works for the *Record Mirror* on my production journalism course, and about the girl on the course whose mum works for that Catholic paper and wonder if I'd like to fuck her, and about flavoured Johnnies and about how expensive driving lessons are and I better pass my test soon and... I couldn't really come and wondered whether I should fake it. Why not?

Friday March 10 1989

I was left wanting and waiting for debauchery. Then when it came it was a huge let down. The speed was god awful, it just kept me awake long enough to speak to lots of people who I didn't want to speak to. And vice versa probably. XXXX freaked out about having AIDS – or so she maybe thought. Paranoid. And the inevitable sex was nothing. Boring even.

Unfulfilled promise, thwarted dreams, having to do it all again.

Tuesday March 28 1989

I'm worried that all my friends have left or are leaving. But I'm here to stay. Worried that what I'm saying is just an exercise in writing and not from the heart. It is. But I can't hear myself. My voice. I am worried then that I am not a writer... drunk with XXXX at the Sonic Youth gig, first at the Warwick Arms down the Portobello Road – XXXX XXXX called my ex, Marlene, a dyke. Yeah. But I still had a go at him. I got beer all over myself somehow.

Saturday April 1 1989

Latin night at the Alexandra, Clapham. Danced with XXXX who asked about XXXX, but still kissed me. Ah who cares? Patrick Walker says 13 aspects (whatever they are) are hurtling into my sign. Can I handle it? Ooh...

Monday April 10 1989

Housing housing housing. Suddenly a note, a phone call, and we're over a grand in arrears. With an eviction notice looming. Panic. Where would I go? Nowhere. Ring N to get her on her housing association list, and onto the council list – pah! Terry is in same position as me.

Wednesday April 19 1989

I just want to sleep in sweet oblivion. I need to be more cheerful – like Tom Jones, he had no friends, no money but a smile *and* a whistle on his lips. And he was pretty. Tom Jones.

Thursday May 11 1989

Went to the Strike Against Art exhibition, or whatever it's called. Better evening than I expected it to be. To the pub with Mark Downham, cold, strange, cerebral – potential psycho? – and Stewart Home – a sniffling type, but strangely more fun than Downham, even though he doesn't drink. Talk about doing a fanzine with Tom to be called *Kick*, same as my old fanzine, which would be weird.

Greil Marcus book *Mystery Train* was sent to me, it looks beautiful. All the Neoist/*Vague* crowd hate him. So what. Interview with Marcus arranged – what to ask him?

Friday September 1 1989

Is something wrong with me? I think about depression, but nothing is wrong, really. It's sunny, shining like a late summer afternoon, like that day Danuta died. Days like this I usually and anxiously wonder what the fuck to do. Today my work is cut out for me – writing about a world that I hardly feel in touch with. Is that it? What? What was I going to say? Interrupted by XXXX on the phone – depressed, wants to smash things, probably her life.

Urgh. I started smoking again.

TV boredom. But the film *Leaving* was... good. About dying and escape and how the future rolls you around, chews you up, puts you down. But I can't afford these feelings. This is reality and I need to immerse myself in the world ... in youth (and you). There is hope in that?

Date Unreadable

Reading the Aleister Crowley *Portable Darkness* anthology – his material and commentary. Fucking impenetrable in general – magic and writing – magic *is* writing. Made very clear. Magic is back. Interesting to know that Crowley prefers the poetic to that didactic – don't we all! But in that case why are the Savages and Marcuses so popular and influential?

Date Unreadable

Richard Hell last night. Crowded with bounding bohos, and cool girls with flowing hair, red lipstick and lust for poetry in their eyes. And shapeless guys with a serious attitude. And how was Hell? Not hellish. Scraggy bowl haircut bum freezer striped suit. Cool in Greenwich Village once maybe. As for the poetry, he introduced it as 'Like Lydia's, but more intellectual, Music for the mind.' Hardly. Most of it was instantly forgettable. All apart from the extreme stuff I suppose – a poem about crime, and 'the first time I ever took junk, I knew that society didn't want ya to have the good stuff (junk) and deep pornography (yuk)' etc. And a couple of poems about butt fucking – 'I parted her cheeks, the anus is rosy, the thing I liked about her was her face and her face was her anus.' That kind of shit. Lapped up by the girls with heads tilted in awe. I wonder if they'd find butt fucking with Hell poetic? I doubt it. I dunno. All these post modern porno art fuckers like – I don't think they know how it really feels like being down at the cheap and nasty end of the scale. I could be wrong. But it seems fake. Anger that expresses itself in disgust,? Yeah well here's anger that expresses itself in bad karma every day... every day.

Outside the gig two girls asked Terry and I to stick with them – some weird guy was hassling them. Maybe for anal sex, who knows. There was almost violence but the guy fucked off.

And we all fucked off.

Diary ends.

×

APPENDIX 1

Positive Punk

Written by Richard Cabut using pen name Richard North, New Musical Express, 19 February 1983.

PART ONE

'Don't dream it, be it.' – *Rocky Horror Show*

The boy sits before the staring mirror and ponders his clean-shaven reflection. Smiling, he selects a carefully-compiled tape and slots it into his machine. *Fatman* is the first track: Southern Death Cult excite him and he dances in his seat while unscrewing a tube of foundation cream.

He's got to look good tonight – and it's becoming every night – because he's off out to a gig. He's going to see one of his bands, one of the groups he regularly sees. Brigandage, Southern Death Cult, Danse Society, Ritual, Rubella Ballet, Virgin Prunes, Specimen, The Mob... They're the only ones that mean anything to him anymore.

Tonight it's Blood and Roses at London's Moonlight Club and all his friends will be there. One of their tracks, *Your Sin is Your Salvation*, comes up on the tape and the boy remembers the last time he saw them.

The blur of colour, the heady atmosphere, the fun, the collective feeling of motion – forward! It made him feel alive, positive, and then he formed a group the next week.

Finishing his make-up the boy turns his attention to his dyed blue hair, carefully back-combing it into disarray. Last week he'd been beaten up by some skinheads because they didn't like the look of him. He remembers their fury but shrugs: he enjoys his appearance and is proud to look different. In a way he's almost glad that his clothes and attitude had provoked the attack – their mindlessness wrapped in a dull, grey, lazy uniform of bitterness gives him a reason to be their opposite.

He feels bright and optimistic about the future, slipping into a pair of leather trousers, noticing he's only got a few quid left in his pocket. It doesn't matter though, the dole gives him time to do things, like his group.

A Brigandage number blares out: Hope, it seems to sum things up for him. With its message on his lips the boy half-dances across the room, through the door and out.

PART TWO

'I don't like the word movement, but there's now a large collection of bands and people with the same positive feeling.' – Andi, singer with Sex Gang Children, speaking on the opening night of Son of Batcave.

Hail Eris, Goddess of Discord, and pass the ammunition: as the heavy drumbeat rolls and the harsh chords crash and sometimes even tingle, it's then that the boys and girls come out to play.

Playpower!

With wild-coloured spiked hair freezing the eye, and even more vivid clothes to spice the imagination – faces, thoughts and actions – the atmosphere's infused with a charge of excitement, an air of abandon underlined with a sense of purpose.

Something stirs again in this land of fetid, directionless sludgery, this land of pretend optimism and grim reality. Theory and practice are being synthesised under the golden umbrella of a 24-hour long ideal.

Welcome to the new positive punk.

Although it's not the purpose of this article to create any kind of movement or cult, any easy or accessible bandwagon to be tumbled onto, it is indisputable that a large number of bands and people involved in the culture called rock, have sprung up at approximately the same time, facing their lifestyles in the same direction. Maybe unconsciously so, it's a huge collective force that we can call the new positive punk – a re-evaluation and rejuvenation of the ideals that made the original outburst so great, an intensification of and expansion of that ethos of individuality, creativity and rebellion. The same buzz that burned our streets, hearts and minds in '76/'77 is happening again.

The Industrial Revolution is over, a new era has begun, and the current mood is an affirmation of that point. The natural energy that for over 200 years has been poured into the physical, the rational and the materialistic, has now all grown crooked. The mental/magical power has been lost: it was simply not needed – steam engines, radios, electricity were so much easier and they worked. But now the glamour is wearing off; we can see the strings and wires, the clockwork squeaks... the radiation is beginning to corrode the pretty box.

All the darkness and light, all the forces are still there deep underneath, bubbling, steaming, fermenting. The instinct, ritual and ceremony are rising again in everyday life; many people are starting to use the tarot and I-Ching. And the new punk groups are a reflection of this feeling; their use of mystical/metaphysical imagery and symbolism is a striking common denominator. Not in the way of dumb-dabbling and superficial posturing of, say, a Black Sabbath with their (gasp) black magic kick.

Nor is it a silly hippy Tolkien fantasy joyride, or even a Killing Joke stench-of-death gloomier-than-thou slice of fanaticism. It is, instead, an intelligent and natural interest in mystery, rather than history, that is a sign of an open mind.

These groups are aware: UK Decay (positive punk forefathers), using the dark to contrast and finally emphasise the light; Sex Gang Children taking us into the sub-world of the Crowleyan abyss; while Blood and Roses are pushing the symbols a whole lot further, their guitarist Bob being a serious student of the Art.

The mystical tide we are talking about here refers, if nothing else, to the inner warmth and vital energy that human beings regard as the most favourable state to live in. The new positive punk has tapped into this current.

And if all this sounds a touch heavy, let's consider the humour, style and inherent fun that are essential parts of the movement. Let's look at groups like Specimen, who are more *Rocky Horror* than Aleister Crowley, preening themselves in a glam-soaked traipse among the ruins. Or The Virgin Prunes' cheeky onstage oral sex send-up. The real humour is intermixed with the sheer sense of *joie de vivre* present at such gatherings.

Here is a glow of energy and life that overcomes the need for artificial stimulation. Unlike the heroin or barbiturate sodden club scene or the glue-swamped Oi/punk arena, the emphasis here is not on drugs. Although illicit substances are not unknown, the desperate desire to nullify boredom is not present, and therefore there is no narcotic edge to the scene. Members of several groups (such as Southern Death Cult, Sex Gang Children and UK Decay) do not even drink.

For perhaps the first time, an active and flourishing dissenting body will not go down with its hind legs kicking as the drug takes over.

Money and time are tight: so both of them are being spent on something far more enjoyable and important: style. There's a veritable explosion of multi-coloured aestheticism. So different from the bland, stereotyped Oi/boot boy punk fare of jeans, leather jacket and studs, this is an individualist stance even if it tends towards a common identity. A green-haired spike-topped girl wearing a long black pleated skirt, white parachute top and bootlace tie passes a tasselled, black-haired mohawk in creepers, white socks, red pegs and self-made, neatly-designed T-shirt. Something clicks. They smile in acknowledgement.

We are fireworks.

PART THREE

'I think that our influence comes from the fact that there are so many negative bands around. We're not – so away we go!' – Bob, guitarist with Blood and Roses, Stoke Newington

If the bands absorb, reflect and present (not necessarily in that order, it's a give and take thing) the attitude of their fans and the tone of their surroundings – and I think that the important ones do – then we can trace the whole thing back to its roots, travelling through the erotic politics of the influential Doors and the tense dusky danger of The Velvet Underground, then we come to The Sex Pistols, who operated under a vicious amalgam of style and direction.

Projecting a perfect combination of distorted but relevant aesthetics, music and suss, their all-important effect was the provocation of thought.

Then, veering away from 1002 misdirected cardboard copies, we come to the Banshees and the Ants. These two are important to the new positive punk: the Banshees because of their sheer power of imagination, and the Ants because of their promotion of sensuous 'black' style.

Both had an adventurous and rebellious air about them that cut through the regressive dross. Their outlook, musically and in angle of thought, went beyond the proscribed boundaries of behaviour at the time. They explored the edges of light and dark and some of the areas in between. They were a progression and they are the two clearest reference points to this recent outburst of energy.

Back at the tail-end of '78 and beyond, punk spun into a tail dive of tuinol-dazed tiredness. A pause. Trends came and want: dead ends such as mod, new romanticism – up to and including the funk craze – all took their toll on the vital energy. And those who stuck with the essence of their punk were faced with the development of Oi! Punk, under the guidance of certain lobots, gathered itself around a banner of no brains, no style, no heart and no hope. Heads buried in the glue-bag of dejection and floundering away under a barrage of three-chord rubbish – this was, and is, no way to lead a life.

Some drifted with the anarcho scene which at the time (1980/81) was the only worthwhile concern going. But by 1983, when everything is said and done, that angle seems too flat and puritan to be of much inspirational value. Crass although anti-sexist, were and still are extremely sexless: a stark, bleak Oliver Cromwell new model army, who have sense but no-sensuality.

At the opposite end of the scale, inspired by the feeling of the Ants etc, come the two groups who are the immediate forerunners of today's flood. They are Bauhaus and, later, Theatre of Hate – both of whom capitalised on the idea of style and, what is more, a dangerous and sensuous style that attracted more and more fans who were sick of the bleak and macho Oi! and the shallow cult with no name.

It's these fans, reacting against the devaluation of punk, and fired by the spirit of the above-mentioned mentors, who are acting now. They've created a colourful and thriving nationwide scene – resplendent in their individuality but still linked by a progressive punk idiom, one that says go instead of stop, expand instead of contract, yes instead of no. A new, positive punk.

PART FOUR

'Stimulating thought, bringing people together, entertaining people, creating an atmosphere of sheer exhilaration and enjoyment. These are the main things.' – Ian, singer with Southern Death Cult, NME 2.10.82

Andi Sex Gang twitches in the spotlight, the beam reflecting his harsh features and closely-cropped hair. He clenches his fists and spits out *Into the Abyss.*

Ian Southern Death Cult flails his arms and chicken-war dances across the stage, a sharp youthful figure with black be-feathered mohawk. His song is *Moya*, the words and the power behind the words providing an insight into cultural stagnation. He howls and shrieks in defiance. Mark from The Mob, and anarcho-renegade, with his bleached dread hair stands up straight before the microphone, growling 'Still living in the English fear, waiting for the witch hunt dear.'

All this and more as Michelle Brigandage leaps onto the amps, top hat at a rackish angle. 'As we walk in the sunlight honesty protects our eyes,' is her cry. And Bob Blood and Roses, he just grins, he knows...*Love is the Law* – their tale underlining the truly optimistic undercurrent to this mood.

And the fans, bedecked in sparkling, inventive garb, they kick, they jump, they scream.

'A night for celebration, a night to unwind,' repeats the diminishing echo from the ghost of UK Decay. 'For celebration, celebration, celebration...'

PART FIVE

'There's nothing else. Everything else has been stripped from us. So now we're just gonna do it. There's no other choice.' – Michelle, singer with Brigandage

So here it is: the new positive punk, with no empty promises of revolution, either in the rock'n'roll sense or the wider political sphere. Here is only a chance of self-awareness, of personal revolution, of colourful perception and galvanisation of the imagination that startles the slumbering mind and body from their sloth.

Certainly this is revolution in the non-political sense, but at the same time it's neither escapist nor defeatist. It is, in fact, 'political' in the genuine sense of the word.

Individuality? Creativity? Rebellion? The synthesis comes at the moment when you do the one thing, the only thing, when you know you're not just a trivial counter on the social chequerboard. Here are thousands doing that one thing: merging an explosive and cutting style with a sense of positive belief and achievement, and having fun while they're doing it.

The Oi-sters and their ilk may have taken punk a few millimetres to the right or a centimetre to the left, but not one damn step forward.

This is punk – at last built on rock and not on sand.

APPENDIX 2

Kick

By Richard Cabut.

In the autumn of 1982, I was living in a punk squat in New North Road, London, N1, a walk from Old Street, unreconstructed and sort of scary/lairy at that time. On one occasion I was mugged for 26-and-a-half pence; all I had in my pocket and pretty much all I had in the world. I was on the dole and spent my time conducting a fruitful lifestyle from what I described in my fanzine *Kick* as 'creativity, individuality and rebellion'.

Kick 4 had been published at the end of that summer and had attracted a fair amount of attention from other fanzines, the music press and even received mention on the *John Peel Show* – which meant a lot. It was the interaction offered by selling the mag at gigs by bands like Southern Death Cult, UK Decay and Sex Gang Children that had led to an invite to live in the squat. *Kick* was part of, and described, a certain scene. As I wrote in the introduction to that issue:-

Although we are pushing PUNK, I think it's become necessary to define terms. For a start, we're not talking about punk in terms of the oi oi, bootboy lot who have nothing to say & nothing to offer. It's their brainless, class, macho mentality that punk has been trying to get rid of from the start. It's 'easy way out' punk that requires a leather jacket for the night and not much else. Then for the rest of the week it's work, pub, death. On the other hand and & at the opposite end of the scale are the 'dead-head' type punx who have seen a fragment of freedom (thru squatting, no work etc.) but have chained themselves up again thru drug dependence and other fixed dogmas & expectations. Self-destruction has become some sort of punk common denominator in a lot of people's minds. But not in ours. We're still conveying it as a positive way of beating reality rather than escaping it (for a few hours down a pub or club). Punk still means the destruction of the conventions and expectations that society has thrown up. It means working on the preconceptions that surround things like work, parents, school, clothes etc. etc. This is why punk is still relevant and important and if you want it to happen, then make it happen for yourself, don't wait for others to do it for you. 'Do it now'. When you do, natural intelligence, instinct & energy will develop thru repeated indulgence. The rebellious surge will transform 'WORK', REST & PLAY into one single conscious and subconscious experiment in LIFE.

In the second part of the introduction, I imagined punks as barbarians at the gates of 'Rome' – their appearance signalling a crisis in civilisation. Punks, I fancied, were part of one of W.B. Yeats' cyclic turns: they were the rough beast slouching towards Bethlehem to be born. I was sure of this. After all, 'mere anarchy' had been loosed. Although there was nothing 'mere' about it as far as I was concerned. I suggested that the current punk sphere had evolved from the 'caper of the Seventies' on to a 'total rejection of the whole of society'. I wrote about how I and some friends in my suburban hometown had always been barbarians, or at least since being first inspired by punk, and had remained so, waiting for the world to catch up with us, to reach a crisis: 'What that crisis is and why the present generation is reacting to it the way it does is the theme of this fanzine and of the issues following it'.

My own crisis had culminated in the flight from suburbia – to London. The bright lights. 'Don't dream it, be it' (*The Rocky Horror Show*). Yeah.

London was, of course, the traditional destination for suburban refugees – people who felt disaffected by life in the sticks: the treadmill, the mores, the conservatism, the repressive nature of family life. We wanted to tip all of this upside down, assert ourselves and fathom the world. In the late '70s and early '80s, there existed a diaspora centred in the capital, where punks sought fresh forms of community. Consequently, social spaces sprang up where punk culture could really develop. The Anarchy Centre, first in Wapping, and then on the Harrow Road, provided a place for extraordinary enveloping happenings. And, Ollie Wisdom's Batcave – before the hoo-ha: a multi-media hang out mixing DJs with cinema and a range of live acts in a fantastically expressive atmosphere where reality could be confronted and perhaps subverted a little.

I lived and gallivanted with some of the people who would later become known as the *Kill Your Pet Puppy* Collective, including Tony

D, who produced the *KYYP* fanzine, first at the aforementioned squat in New North Rd, and then in Westbere Road, West Hampstead. The New North Road squat broke up thanks to petty animosities and personality clashes. The house was later taken over by Tom Vague and friends, and my room was inhabited by Ian, singer of The Southern Death Cult, later The Cult, who drew some pretty funky drawings all over the walls.

The place I moved to in West Hampstead was something of hub. All kinds of cool and crazy people would pitch up. Bands, writers, vagrants, and a TV crew on occasion. It was a punk rock melting pot of striking creativity and cross-pollination. The interaction fuelled creativity and vice versa. 'Westbere Road was a sanctuary from the changes sweeping punk at the time,' Tony D recalled. 'It was also a catalyst'.

In Westbere Road, and other punk squats, a young, rebellious, open culture began to create (mostly mayhem!). An honourable, self-sufficing and self-sufficient economy – low-level capitalism – began, based on the production of music, fanzines, fashion and art. Squats became hives of activity for a diverse range of people. It was a world away from both suburban restraint and urban bedsit boredom, or from the lifestyle of the aforementioned 'dead-head type punx' in their seedy, down 'n' out squats.

Blood and Roses' Bob Short in his book *Filth* portrays this scene best, perhaps. Bob accurately describes how life was really lived – and death really died – in extreme conditions of debauch and poverty underpinned by a sense of overwhelming stare-at-the-wall-drooling boredom, punctuated only by outbursts of violence and furore, usually fuelled by whatever substances came to hand. It's an underworld of alienation, loneliness, hopelessness and anger. Well, it was either that or get a job ...

Short's London was centred in the Campbell Buildings in Waterloo, a kind of punk annex to Dante's inferno, a nether place peopled in the main by 'dole bludgers, charlatans, delinquents, drug addicts, petty thieves and musicians.' The worst, of course, were the musicians and therein lies the link between squalor and glamour, I suppose.

A similar hellhole was to be found at Coronation Buildings in

Vauxhall, home for a while of *Kick* writer Lill. I remember visiting once to find scenes of devastation after a roving gang of skinheads had attacked the squat and raped some of the female punks. In *Kick*, though, I very much accentuated the positive. I liked the punk scene in the early '80s. I liked it in the mid-1970s too. The late-70s, though, were like the third Monday in January, officially recognized by the medical profession as the day on which more UK citizens wake up depressed than any other. The reality of another grinding year kicks in, the horror of the Christmas credit card bill bites, and the misery of another rain dashed day dawns. It was like that. But the early '80s were another punk spring. As described, punk at that time became a way of life for an increasingly large and motivated group of people. Moreover, folk were, to paraphrase Malcolm McLaren, creating an environment in which they could truthfully run wild. Instead of just listening to records in isolation and going to the odd gig, people were having life adventures – documented by fanzines like *KYPP* (the biggest and best fanzine), *Panache, Vague* and *Kick*.

We wrote about bands like Southern Death Cult, Sex Gang Children, Bauhaus, their predecessors Adam and the Ants and the Banshees, and later Brigandage and Blood and Roses: bands that promulgated the overriding ethic and aesthetic of rebellion, individuality and creativity, with a touch of esoterica, some flash and plenty of glam dash to boot. Having said that, the music was the least important part of the equation – the bands simply provided the soundtrack to a lifestyle.

We strutted our Billy-the-Kid sense of cool – bombsite kids clambering from the ruins – posing our way out of the surrounding dreariness. We were living in our own colourful movie (an early-ish Warhol flick some of us liked to think), which we were sure was incomparably richer, more spontaneous and far more magical than the depressing, collective black-and-white motionless picture that the conformists had to settle for. But we had a clear understanding of the here and now, and a desire to get out of it – rather than just get out of it. We cared with unflinching sincerity, although not many were intellectuals or activists in the traditional political sense. Of more interest were, perhaps, the fantastic slogans. 'They said that oblivion was their ruling passion. They wanted to reinvent everything each day; to become the masters of their own lives.' That kind of thing. And I don't recall many people attending marches or 'political' meetings on a regular basis.

I once wrote a sort of verse, which talked about the 'Romance of Anarchy' becoming 'Reality'. I believed that the romance is grounded in a reality that makes clear that, on all levels, the process of daily life is based on a trade of humiliations and aggro, as the Situationists (a big influence, of course) said. I thought that 'alienated work is a scandal', that so-called 'leisure' is an affront, and that 'real life is elsewhere.' Where? Well, the pertinent questions, I thought, are not about restructuring economic systems, although I admit on a day-to-day level that helps, but about how quickly the underpinnings of society – all the givens, great unmentionables, so-called axioms, the fact that it is a closed-loop feedback system which easily sops up and throws back challenges and critiques – could be dissolved. I demanded that this happens. And I felt, to paraphrase the Situ slogan and Malcolm McLaren's shirt, I was entirely reasonable to demand the impossible.

This, I feel, was the overriding, if sometimes coded, message given in the best fanzines of those years. Including *Kick*, I hope. My fanzine, and the scene itself, to an extent, was probably more influenced by someone like Richard Neville and his 'Politics of Play.' In his 1970 book, *Playpower*, Neville stands aside from the straight Left. We got the memo. The straights were about working hard and supportively, while for us there was no wish to work at all. The straights wanted work for everyone (and this was a time of mass unemployment) whereas we shrugged off the very thought of routine to focus on the exciting stuff, and somehow managed to get by.

We were like kids (hence *Play*power). I was positive that self-empowered, autodidactic, spiky guttersnipes were an upsurge of the future, certain to overcome the old political order – the RCP, the SWP, the stolid Left, the more traditional anarchists even. I remember, later, sneering at the people who supported the miners' strike. Many in our circle did. I remember talking to Fred Vermorel, author of *Sex Pistols: The Inside Story* amongst other books, who moaned about the Pistols' art director Jamie Reid because he spoke out in support of the strike. We wondered why anyone would want to work underground. I regret this attitude now. We should all have stood firm. This is clearly the downside of the so-called 'cult of individuality' – politically, a liberal dead end, to paraphrase writer Marek Kohn.

Instead, *Kick* and the other fanzines described the punk scene in the same way as, in one episode of the TV show *Bewitched*, the character Endora describes the difference between witches and humans, 'They all look the same to me, noses to the grindstone shoulders to the wheel, feet planted firmly on the ground, no wonder they can't fly!' She adds: 'It's fine for them but not for us. We are quicksilver, a fleeting shadow, a distant sound that has no boundaries through which we can't pass. We are found in music, in a flash of colour, we live in the wind and in a sparkle of star...'

It was a magical time, in more ways than one. Serious, sometimes seemingly endless conversations were held about occultists like Aleister Crowley, Austin Osman Spare, Kenneth Grant and the possibilities of magic. Use of the tarot and I Ching were a daily occurrence. The inside back cover of *Kick 4* was a hastily drawn Tree of Life – from Kether to Malkuth. 'Magic hung in the air', Tony D recalled, 'life was almost unexplainable and the only way to make sense of it was through people like Crowley and his works and path.'

Few, though, ploughed through the theory. Most were more interested in the mystery rather than the history, I suppose. As Kohn wrote in his 1983 'Punk's new Clothes' piece for *The Face*: 'Two things in rock are really easy to conjure up without trying very hard: a loud noise and an air of mystery. For the latter, you just drop a few hints and your audience fall over themselves to do the rest. A lack of irony, playfulness and humour; a handful of horror images (both the supernatural and the violent varieties), a need to conjure up an aura...'

But there was a little more to the association between magic and our punk scene than that, as I myself wrote in the *NME* in 1983:

'Nor is it a silly hippy Tolkien fantasy joyride, or even a Killing Joke stench-of-death gloomier-than-thou slice of fanaticism. These groups are aware: UK Decay (positive punk forefathers), using the dark to contrast and finally emphasise the light; Sex Gang Children taking us into the sub-world of the Crowleyan abyss; while Blood And Roses are pushing the symbols a whole lot further, their guitarist Bob being a serious student of the Art. The mystical tide we are talking about here refers, if nothing else, to the inner warmth and vital energy that human beings regard as the most favourable state to live in. The new positive punk has tapped into this current.'

I started writing for the *NME* towards the end of 1982. This was probably one of the reasons why *Kick 5* was never printed, although I had already put together much of that issue. Echoing the 1960s/70s exodus of writers from the underground press to the mainstream, I jumped on the music press bandwagon, as did many of the main punk fanzine writers: Tom Vague (*Vague–ZigZag*), Mick Mercer (*Panache–Melody Maker*), Alistair Livingston (*The Encyclopaedia of Ecstasy–Punk Lives*), Tony D (*Kill Your Pet Puppy–NME*), Robin Gibson (*It Ticked and Exploded–Sounds*). Why? The consensus amongst ourselves was that we had 'sold out' in order to further push 'our' bands and 'the revolution'. We felt that we were, with our undying passion for punk, attacking orthodoxy and challenging those in power, sometimes in volatile ways. We thought we were encouraging the overground music press to tackle concerns that they would otherwise have ignored – for instance, I wrote about the Black Sheep Housing Co-op, which grew out of the squatting movement in Islington (I was a member). Tony D wrote about international anarchist organisations for the *NME* and Alistair Livingston wrote about the Anarchy Centre for *Punk Lives.*

But we also revelled in the attention and status that an *NME* by-line attracted and afforded. I remember the moment I decided I would try to join the *NME*, during a conversation with Tony about the merits of some LP. Tony, who had already taken the IPC shilling, countered my no-doubt excellent argument with, 'Pah, *you* don't write for the *NME*'. I soon did – Tony was to blame. Despite the fact that we had all sniped at the *NME* in our fanzines, we regarded it, in truth, with no little respect.

I wrote the positive punk article for the *NME* in January–February 1983. Really, it reiterated much of what I had previously written in *Kick*, and what other fanzines had reported, too, about the state of the punk scene in the early 80s. At that time there were three distinct groupings. The Oi-sters and 'herberts', who were basic and gumby-ish in their music, fashion and behaviour; the anarchos, who were a mass of black, in terms of clothes and demeanour; and our loose, nameless collection of punks and former punks who were colourful and full, it seemed, of vim and go-ahead spirit. We tended to go to see roughly the same bands and attended the same sort of clubs. I wrote about many of the bands and places, ranging from the Batcave and Specimen to The Mob (who were sort of anarcho-plus). I liked the make-up-break-down, safe-when-dangerous, follow-the-heart-and-unconscious-mind, heaven-and-hell-and-kiss-and-tell bands like Bauhaus, Wasted Youth, Flesh for Lulu and Psychedelic Furs. Groups that promoted sensual style and re-action: 'With wild-coloured spiked hair freezing the eye, and even more vivid clothes to spice the imagination – faces, thoughts and actions – the atmosphere's infused with a charge of excitement, an air of abandon underlined with a sense of purpose. Something stirs again in this land of fetid, directionless sludgery, this land of pretend optimism and grim reality. Theory and practice are being synthesised under the golden umbrella of a 24-hour long ideal. Welcome to the new positive punk [...] a re-evaluation and rejuvenation of the ideals that made the original outburst so great, an intensification of and expansion of that ethos of individuality, creativity and rebellion.'

The positive punk article garnered a reaction. *Melody Maker* wrote an amusing pastiche; *The Face* replied with its own piece complete with photos of all the key participants; there were myriad mentions in the fanzines; LWT's Friday night arts and leisure series, *South of Watford*, devoted an episode to the 'movement'. Host Michael Moorcock came to Westbere Road one morning to conduct interviews and, seeing that we were all worse for wear after a late night at the Tribe Club, gave us some (extremely potent) speed to encourage the chat. It worked … perhaps all too well – *Private Eye* contacted me afterwards to ask whether it was true that the presenter had given drugs to his obviously over-refreshed interviewees. I denied everything.

But Positive Punk was a disaster. Once something is named, it becomes easy to attack. Bands like Sex Gang Children refused to become involved – because they couldn't control it. Their noses had been put out of joint. The big wigs in the scene, Sex Gang, Southern Death Cult, *et al*, had suddenly been usurped, or so they thought, by upstarts like Brigandage and Blood and Roses, who had received most coverage in the piece. Overnight, the atmosphere changed from togetherness to suspicion, jealousy and loathing. This would probably have happened in any case, but the article greatly accelerated the process. As far as I am concerned, positive punk described the 'Passage of a few People (wearing makeup and top hats) through a Rather Brief Moment in Time.' I think it was accurate. In hindsight, the music wasn't great but, as aforesaid, that wasn't really the point. And then it turned into goth, with even worse music.

The Westbere Road house also finished – many of the *KYPP* collective went off to become New Age Travellers. I, meanwhile, joined Brigandage and continued to write for the music press and, later, various national media organisations. Nevertheless, I maintain that *Kill Your Pet Puppy*, *Vague*, *Kick* and the other fanzines of that time and space, revealed our particular genre of '80s punk to be remarkable in its essence – creative, spirited and progressive. Full of, yes, individuality, creativity and rebellion.

X

APPENDIX 3

1977

By Richard Cabut.

In the summer of 1977, I am seventeen – perfect.

I don't work. Although I washed cars for a week once when my mate Steve went on holiday. The boss said they'd be cleaner if he'd pissed on them. Fuck off, baldy.

I speed a bit – little brown packets tucked in zip pockets – and do other stuff, too. Inspired by the Ramones and Mark P, I try sniffing glue, but it doesn't work for me. I open the tin, take a tentative little snifflet of Cow Gum and am surprised when nothing happens – little do I realise that you have to tip the stuff in a plastic bag and stick it over your head for five minutes before you can satisfactorily fall flat on your face, off your napper. They should print clear, precise instructions in the punk zines for God's sake.

I also occasionally indulge in over-the-counter decongestants. Do-Dos. One tablet per day is the recommended dose. So I take eight and get a buzz. Wait. If I feel a mild hit on eight then, well, what if I take thirty? I'll feel really good, right? I vomit for a whole day and feel like shit for the next three. But this doesn't stop me from going through the whole process all over again a few weeks later. And so on. Seventeen...

Mostly I dream of escape. I live in small-town, working/lower-middle-class suburbia. Dunstable, Bedfordshire. Thirty miles from the capital. Here, kids leave school and go on the track, the production line, at the local factory, Vauxhall Motors. If you get some qualifications you can join the civil service. Meanwhile, Trevor and Nancy have been going out with each other since third form and watch telly round each other's house every night, not saying a word. I don't know what I want, but I know I don't want any of that shit ever.

Instead, I'm in love with punk rock. I'm in love with picking up momentum and hurling myself forward somewhere. Anywhere. Rip up the pieces and see where they land. I am suburban-punk Everykid in pins and zips, with a splattering of Jackson Pollock and a little Seditionaries – getting chased down the King's Road, after bunking the train down to the Smoke, by (strangely) American rednecks rather than Teddy Boys, although that does happen too (the Rasta at the antiques market, Troy his name is, hands out cut-throat razors to harassed punks). And wraparound shades worn after dark so that everything is but murk, which might explain a heavy snogging session that turns out to be same-sex – rolling about on the stage while the Damned are playing. Divine decadence, I like to think.

I write my first fanzine, *Corrugated Boredom* (which later becomes Kick), pondering pretentiously on Dada and Surrealism, and penning bad poetry. Hey, luckily I still have some around. Here's one: 'You live in a coffin / You can't move / You're buried alive / You've done it to yourself / What can you do? / Before, you wanted life / Now you just want existence' – which I actually read out live. You get the picture.

I also bash away on an old four-string acoustic guitar and write crappy, clichéd songs. I remember one: 'Blades for flowers / drainpipes for jeans / Hippies are dead / and they'll never return / 67 reversed has destroyed that dream.' It's actually written the year before, in the summer of 76, after seeing Dr Feelgood (mid- set, Captain Sensible crept up behind Lee Brilleaux and gave him a mighty two-handed shove into the audience. What a wag). But is obviously inspired by the Pistols – whose gig at the Leighton Buzzard Bossard Hall in the summer off 77 is unfortunately banned that very afternoon when I turn up to see them.

Meanwhile, in my bedroom there's *Sniffin' Glue and Other Self-Defence Habits* (July 77), some Aleister Crowley, a bit of Sartre, *48 Thrills* (bought off Adrian at a Clash gig), Sandy Roberton's *White Stuff* (from Compendium in Camden) and John Peel, of course.

And tons of records – I love the smell of fresh new punk vinyl, as well as the slightly different scent of Jamaican imports (pressed on old recycled vinyl, because of cheapness rather than eco awareness) – all of it a shining, odorous promise of unexpected imaginings. It smells of the future. Can't wait till 78? Definitely. The intensity of sitting in a loud room in a silent town, full of electricity. Floating above circumstances. Soaring...

...and flicking V-signs during the Jubilee itself, while nicking Union flags from wherever they can be found (everywhere), and invariably hanging out in the Ladies' (à la the Roxy Club) – although this has repercussions. But local reaction is bemusement rather than hatred. There's only a handful of punks in town; no threat. There's also a certain amount of crossover anyway. Skiz, who was there at the Clash Rainbow gig, is still into football aggro: at Luton v Fulham, he fights it out with a Londoner, who is also a punk. A weird feeling, says Skiz, who shouts: 'He's got a knife!' – and even a nearby copper starts putting the boot in on the Fulham fan. And everyone is still into funk, too: the California Ballroom is Dunstable's equivalent of the Lacy Lady or Global Village. Since 75 or so, hip kids had been travelling from miles around (even from London) for the plastic sandals and pegs scene there. It was all quite retro – Forties swing fashions – until punk.

The real hatred around my way comes early in the following year, in 1978. That's when all the truly rough and tough kids from the surrounding London-overspill estates get into punk for a couple of months or so. On the way to another Clash gig, on 25 January, Steve and I join a big group of new punks, maybe thirty or forty strong, walking along the main road. A police car stops us, and everyone waits his or her turn to be searched. The kid in front of me surreptitiously pulls out a gun, a real revolver that he's nicked from a party, apparently, and passes it back through the group to a girl who sticks it in her handbag, crosses the road and walks away. I should have done the same. The gig itself is a bloodbath. Different estates slug it out with each other – Lewsey Farm v Stopsley – people stagger around with axe wounds, blood everywhere, the Wild West. A support band called the Lou's gets killed, the Sex Pistols' minder Steve English wanders around with a knife. I'm backstage and the Clash are worried: they're popping Mogadons (a downer). I'm worried, too – that I'll get stuck forever in all this bollocks. I know it's time to move. Which I do – to London. And, as it's obligatory to say in pieces like this, I'm still moving.

X

SELECT BIBILIOGRAPHY

The following books were important/essential to me (and to the characters) during the period covered in *Looking for a Kiss* – 1984-89. The selection is confined to those books which I still own – i.e. those which I had access to while writing (books are for touching/feeling). I've listed them in the same order as they are arranged on my shelves.

Jean Genet – *Our Lady of the Flowers*

Friedrich Nietzsche – *Ecce Homo: How One Becomes What One Is* (The chapter titles rock: 'Why I Am So Wise', 'Why I Am So Clever' 'Why I Write Such Good Books' and 'Why I Am a Destiny' etc)

Kenneth Grant – *Aleister Crowley and the Hidden God*

Albert Camus – *The Fall*

Dave Wallis – *Only Lovers Left Alive*

Robert Anton Wilson – *Illuminatus* trilogy (The most interesting thing about SF, some would say, is its dystopian drift. The genre twitches if not bulges with works containing a pulse-pounding progressive inclination complete with overarching themes that speak of anxieties about and enthusiasms for the unravelling of society. Eschewing pseudo rationality and techno fetishism such works deal not so much with prediction, but instead hold a mirror up to the present. Radical ideas are applied to fantastic narratives by writers like Orwell, Dick, and Dave Wallis (*Only Lovers Left Alive*). But the grooviest, hottest and horniest of these is surely Robert Anton Wilson, high and fly and way too wet to dry. I met Wilson in the early 80s, when he was living in Dublin. He told me the city suited him because the four faces of the town hall clock each presented a different time. People called it the Four Liars. This chimed with Bob's sense of humour and philosophical outlook. 'I do not believe in anything but I have my suspicions,' he once said. Wilson's most rigorous attack on the dogmatism of 'reality' – one of his mottos was 'Beware of the Dogma' – came via the 800-page epic the *Illuminatus* trilogy (1975). This is a potted history of the world and a searing assault on the tricksy savagery of politicians and politics. The sprawling structure is underpinned by anything that can be used for fun and kicks – drugs, the occult, sex, and conspiracy theory. It's a riot of dissonance and discord. Very funny with it, though. One reviewer called it 'a fairy story for paranoiacs.' But fairy tales can teach us what text books can't – about the power of mystery and about how reason and logic are not the be all. In *Illuminatus* Wilson slugs it out in the artistic and philosophical arena, drawing on Burroughs, Joyce, Crowley, Ginsberg, Bakunin *et al* in the tussle between convention and progress, the citizen and the state, the Man and men. Not to mention the hepcats and the deadbeats, the solid senders and the squares and the Righteous and the rotten. It's an eternal fight. In the late 70s and early 80s I most encountered *Illuminatus* in the punk squats, crash pads and art labs around London town, in the hands of those on the margins looking for some action and magic.)

Anne Kavan – *Ice* ('What I saw had no solidity, it was all made of mist and nylon, with nothing behind.')

Antonin Artaud – *Artaud Anthology* (Given to me in the 70s by my late cousin, Peter, who, I thought, had a touch of the Artaud about him, and he thought the same about me – that was a little worrying, but I guess we all go through our Antonin A period, no?)

Samuel Beckett – *Molloy*

Susan Sontag – *On Photography*

Virginia Woolf – *To the Lighthouse*

Patti Smith – *Ha! Ha! Houdini!*, *Witt*, *The Night* (with Tom Verlaine) – (I bought all of these one afternoon in the summer of 1976 from

Compendium Books in Camden. I had spent the morning at the Oval watching the West Indies thrash England. I wasn't a cricket fan, so I'm not sure what I was doing there. But I remember the atmosphere was great – more like a raucous football match. The Patti Smith books were pretty cool, too. On the same visit I also bought one or two issues of the great reggae fanzine *Pressure Drop*.)

Henry Miller – *Sexus, Plexus, Nexus*

Colin Wilson – *The Occult* (everyone's 1970s entrée into mysticism. Mine included. Wilson's value lay in his ability to write clearly, concisely yet passionately about subjects that seldom received such treatment. Without resorting to boring 'easy way to learn' methods he put topics like the sexual impulse, mysticism and psychology at the layman's fingertips. Wilson was a pop writer. Pop was cool. Pop is cool.)

Brett Easton Ellis – *Less than Zero, Rules of Attraction* ("Nothing. Nothing makes me happy. I like nothing,' I tell her.')

Danny Sugerman – *Wonderland Avenue: Tales of Glamour and Excess* (' 'Life in the fast lane'... 'What a fucking joke. Everyone knows there are no lanes in a demolition derby.")

William Hughes – *Performance* (The book of the film, which made for astonishing viewing at Scala cinema all-nighters – a place renown for action off screen as well as on).

Eve Babitz – *Slow Days, Fast Company* ('No one burned hotter than Eve Babitz. Possessing skin that radiated 'its own kind of moral laws,")

Cookie Mueller – *Walking Through Clear Water*

Kathy Acker – *Blood and Guts in High School* (I wasn't sure about KA – but I liked her rawness and honesty. She never seemed to be out simply to shock; her subject matter was her natural vision. Her streets were gutters and the kids played at junky and whore instead of Cowboy and Indian, as they say.)

Knut Hamsun – *Hunger* Emmett Grogan – *Ringolevio*

Aleister Crowley – *Confessions of Aleister Crowley, Moonchild, Diary of a Drug Fiend, Book of Thoth*

Fred and Judy Vermorel – *Sex Pistols: The Inside Story, Starlust* (I liked Fred, but we had our misunderstandings at one time. I was going to, with Jane Suck, co-write a front cover *Time Out* piece on Fred until he learned about my involvement and nixed it. But I eventually forgave him.)

Raymond Chandler – Everything

Alexander Baron – *Lowlife*

Charles Bukowski – *Post Office, Ham on Rye, You Get so Alone at Times* ('I wasn't much of a petty thief. I wanted the whole world or nothing.')

Joe Orton – *The Orton Diaries*

Greil Marcus – *Lipstick Traces* (Great launch, or what I can remember of it!)

William Burroughs Jnr – *Speed*

Jim Carroll – *Basketball Diaries*

Martin Millar – *Milk, Sulphate and Alby Starvation*

Guy Debord – *The Society of the Spectacle*

Mervyn Peake – *Gormenghast* trilogy

Andy Warhol – *Popism, The Philosophy of, Diaries of*

Barry Miles – *Ginsberg*

William Gibson – *Burning Chrome, Neuromancer*

JG Ballard – *Concrete Island*

Diane di Prima – *Memoirs of a Beatnik*

Hermine Demoriane – *The Tightrope Walker* (She popped around to my flat once, unannounced. I had no idea how she'd got my address. People used to do that sort of thing in the 80s. We had tea and talked about Derek Jarman, Jean Luc-Godard (she'd interviewed him) and punk. Tightrope walking didn't come up.)

Milton – *Paradise Lost*

Raymond Carver – *What We Talk About When We Talk About Love*

Mick Farren – *Watch Out Kids*

Jay McInerney – *Bright Lights, Big City*

Colin McCabe – *Godard: Images, Sounds, Politics*

Jan Cremer – *I, Jan Cremer* (For a while I played in a band called Woman (with one of the original members of King Kurt, amongst others). Our best song was *I'm Here to Stay*, a paean to the wild Beatnik artist Cremer)

James Joyce – *Ulysses* (I studied English Literature at the Polytechnic of North London, radical hotbed of revolt in the 70s. I took little away from this experience, apart from a poor degree and, far more importantly, a love and appreciation of this book.)

Jean Stein – *Edie* (AW's only real superstar, perhaps, beautiful and doomed, poor little rich girl, an emblem of the Sixties, she was 'an American dream and an American nightmare'. We see her ravaged and polluted: 'Like all great American stories, Edie's is about being born in paradise and then being ejected from it.'

John Berger – *Ways of Seeing*

Roland Barthes – *Mythologies*

Richard Yates – *Revolutionary Road, Cold Spring Harbor* (The perceptive and disturbing *CSH* was Richard Yates' last – it doesn't quite match the stark genius of his great suburban tragedy *Revolutionary Road* but reprises many of the same themes and motifs. So, more unhappy families from an author whose bleak world is marked by sadness, suffocation and the notion that everything is going to end in heart-rending sobs.

The characters face divorce, alcoholism, adultery and mental illness. Like Raymond Carver, Yates cuts at the ordinary veneer of small-town America to expose the claustrophobia underneath.

Despite the surface simplicity of his calm, clean prose there are swirling undercurrents. People marry too young, sperate too quickly and start drinking far too early in the day. Others face the dreadful truths of their failures and inadequacies, while silently longing for love or simply the chance to escape.)

William Burroughs – *Junky*

Richard Neville – *Playpower*

Jim Dodge – *Not Fade Away*

Jeffrey Bernard – *Low Life* (The only reason to read *The Spectator*,

The Sunday Mirror or thinking-man's-freebie *Midweek* in the 80s was for the Soho drunk's Low Life column – 'a suicide note written in weekly instalments'. Tony D and I wasted so much time in those same Soho pubs – Tony said: 'If I saved all the money that I spent on drink, I'd spend it on drink.' I think he nicked that off someone else. Probably Bernard.)

Jean Paul Sartre – *Roads to Freedom*

Nelson Algren – *Never Come Morning, Neon Wilderness* and *A Walk on the Wild Side* (Never play cards with a man called Doc. Never eat at a place called Mom's. Such is the invaluable advice given in Nelson Algren's cult classic of the stricken street, populated by 'lonesome monsters' and not-so-beautiful losers.

A long, loopy hymn to the depression-era underclass. *A Walk on the Wild Side* follows the misfortunes of hapless hobo Dove Linkhorn, defiler of women, who flees Texas for New Orleans. Here, he soon discovers, there's always room for one more at the bottom. Hustlers, prostitutes, pimps and flim-flam men abound as Linkhorn tries to make it as a con man, condom maker and peep-show performer.

Merging profundity and slapstick, Marxist polemic and social surrealism, Algren shoots sparks through the city's French quarter. Less of a traditional narrative and more like a poetic force of nature. *Wild Side* is a boisterous panegyric to the side-street solitaries and who dream their impossible dreams.)

Ed Sanders – Tales of Beatnik Glory

Peter York – *Style Wars*

GI Gurdjieff – *Meetings with Remarkable Men*

Andrew Arato – *Essential Frankfurt School Reader*

Ingmar Bergman – *Scenes from a Marriage*

George Bataille – *Blue of Noon* (George Bataille is the master of abstract erotica-noir. *The Story of the Eye, Madame Edwards* and *L'Anus Solaire* are classics from the Surrealist era – when Bataille formed his own personal movement, attacking with iconoclastic fury both the Surrealists and their enemies alike.

Blue of Noon is a strange broken tale of twisted love set against the background of French café-intellectualism, the general strike in Barcelona and the assassination of Dolphus – events and attitude that were soon eclipsed by greater historical crises.

Bataille's themes, though, are timeless. The two most powerful gods in his mythology are death and eroticism. They are bound to one another. In *Blue of Noon*, eroticism is not simply sex, but sex detached from the reproductive function, driving its energies towards creative form and sensation. In the elaboration of erotic feeling, which appears as the source of individual culture and judgement, many elements come into play. The roles of which must be understood in terms of the human continuum – death, suffering, etc.

Ostensibly *Blue of Noon* is Bataille's 'overtly political' novel. Yet it transcends dogma and, indeed, theory. His approach to the sex/death/power situation brings to mind the more instinctive aspects of de Sade. Like de Sade, Bataille wants 'everything' and 'all at once', which is to want the 'impossible'. But that, as Austryn Wainhouse (English translator of de Sade's *Juliette*), points out, is what the revolution is; the desiring of the impossible, the striking for fulfilment of the impossible desire and anything else is nothing.

Bataille wants what no mere formal rearrangements can provide, what no modification of material and relative conditions can alone satisfy. He wants 'a permanent insurrection of the spirit', an intimate revolution, a revolution within. He wants to change wo/man. To change her/him drastically. Destroying all that which has made relations between all wo/man ... and has merged love and continuity into one disaster.)

Victor Bockris – *The Life and Death of Andy Warhol, Up- Tight: Velvet Underground Story*

Alexander Trocchi – *Young Adam*

Tom Vague – *Vague* 21: Cyber Punk (Wherein techno-street types cut together a science-fiction/critical theory crossover in the post-Situationist techno-cultural fragmentation, the architecture of entropy. Yeah, we're on an express elevator to hell, and we haven't even paid our fare...
...there's S. Home's Richard Allen-style *Skinhead Joins Class War* short story. And Mark Downham's playfully analytical treatise on Cyber-punk.
There's also some original Jamie Reid artwork on the cover, which on its own was worth the price (£4 originally). And while we're on a Pistol's tack, the comprehensive Jon Savage interview acts as a sort of introduction to *England's Dreaming*. The reprint of Sav's 76 fanzine *London's Outrage* shows that even then he was a bit of a smart ass.)

Isabelle Collin Dufresne (Ultra Violet) – *Famous for 15 Minutes*

Dorothy Parker – *The Portable Dorothy Parker*

John Wyndham – *Day of the Triffids*

John Christopher – *Death of Grass*

Paul Sieveking – *Man Bites Man: The Scrapbook of an Edwardian Eccentric* (I went around his house once, you know. Fascinating chap. Ex-editor of the *Fortean Times*, amongst other wonderful things – such as producing the first English translation of Raoul Vaneigem's *The Revolution of Everyday Life*)

Pauline Reage – *Story of O*

Gerald Kersh – *Night and the City*

Lenny Bruce – *The Essential Lenny Bruce* (We had something of a renaissance of hard 'alternative comedy' on our hands with 'crazies' like

Sam Kinneson and Gerry Sadowitz. Their outrageous nature harkened all the way back to the Sick Comic himself, Lennie Bruce – also called the Sickest of the Sick ,The Crown Prince of Dope, The Man From Outer Taste. Reason enough to love him right there – another was his finding a single comprehensive metaphor for human experience. One that stripped away all the lies.)

The Underground Film Bulletin (American mag boldly exploring an 'otherwise invisible film underground', the Bulletin outlines the aesthetics of what is calls 'the cinema of transgression' – nothing less than the destruction of the so-called avant garde ethos which still encourages the traditional formula of unrestricted tedium through unedited sloppiness.

TUFB 5 discusses the idea of Kurt Kern and Otto Muehl. There are also interviews with Lech Kowalski (*DOA* fame) and John Spacely, director and star of *Gringo*, while shiteaters everywhere will adore a comic strip written by Lydia Lunch.)

Marquis de Sade – *Justine, Juliette*

Phillip K Dick – *Ubik*

Anthony Burgess – *Clockwork Orange*

Stephen Koch – *Stargazer* (I reviewed this one for the *NME*, and wrote something like: this pins Warhol down in the underground of the Duchampian *avant garde. Edie, Popism* etc may be the great anecdotal documentaries of the era, but *Stargazer* is a fine analysis of the madness which pulsed through the Factory like a heartbeat. The Factory, a spectacle created from various strands of themes that Warhol's films actually balance on. Withdrawal, passivity and inauthenticity. If Warhol could make his peace with all this, others could not – the casualty list was long. As Koch notes, though, Warhol's 'avenging demon' turned out to be not suicide but murder. In effect Valerie Solanas did not fail. The gaunt master of the passive spectacle was stopped short... Shortly afterwards, the *NME* junked its book reviews page – the downward curve had begun.)

Mark P – *The Bible*

Dennis Morris – *Rebel Rock* (Reminds us that it was/is the idea of the Sex Pistols that was/is important: 'Believe In the Ruins' 'Only Anarchists Are Pretty' (this is true) and ... 'The Only Notes That Matter Are the Ones that Come in Wads.')

Rapid Eye 7/8 – (Imaginative journal of what they called 'de-control'. A penetrating insight into work/mind of Derek Jarman, a comprehensive Burroughs interview by Vale of Re/Search. The inside cover is by Warhol, and the Psychic TV overview is illuminating. Can a price (£5 originally) be put on inspiration?)

Nat Finkelstein – *Andy Warhol*

Jamie Reid – *Up they Rise* (I asked Jamie to sign my copy: 'I owe it all to you, Richard' He didn't seem too pleased, but wrote it all the same.)

William Powell – *Anarchist Cookbook*

ACKNOWLEDGEMENTS AND CREDITS

Used by kind permission: Positive Punk – Copyright Richard Cabut – originally published in the *New Musical Express*, February 1983. Kick – Copyright Richard Cabut – originally published in *Ripped, Torn and Cut*, edited by Matt Worley *et al* (Manchester University Press, 2018). 1977 – Copyright Richard Cabut – originally published in *3:AM Magazine*, 2007. Photographs – Cover image of Richard Cabut and p.14, p.80, p.116 Joan Geoffroy, Copyright Mick Mercer. Images on p.4, p.64, p.71, 132, Copyright Richard Cabut Archive, p.72 photo by Peter Cabut copyright Richard Cabut Archive. Cover image of Anna-Livia Lowendahl and p.46 – Anders Peterson. Thank you: Pete Webb, Cathi Unsworth, Zak and Laura, Malcolm Paul, PT Madden, Sandy Wilson, Jeff Young, Manchester University Press.

×

AUTHOR'S BIBLIOGRAPHY

Richard Cabut is the author of the book *Looking for a Kiss* (PC-Press, 2023, previously Sweat Drenched Press, 2020) and *Disorderly Magic and Other Disturbances* (Far West Press, 2023).

He also authored the chapbook *Deja Vu, Deja Me, Deja You* (Between Shadows Press, 2021) and the novella *Dark Entries* (Cold Lips Press, 2019).

Richard is the co-editor/writer of the anthology *Punk is Dead: Modernity Killed Every Night* (Zer0 Books, October 2017).

And contributor to *Ripped, Torn and Cut – Pop, Politics and Punk Fanzines From 1976* (Manchester University Press, 2018) and to the anthologies *The Edgier Waters* (Snowbooks, 2006), *Affinity* (67 Press, 2015) and *Growing Up With Punk* (Nice Time, 2018).

He was a Pushcart Prize nominee 2016 for the short story *All I Want.* and participant in the Brockley and Lewisham Literary Festival 2022.

Richard's literary pieces have featured in *Paris Bitter Hearts Spring* magazine, *Intellectual Refuge, Laurahird.com, 3AM Magazine, Zouch, Descent.*

He was a textual/visual contributor to the art exhibition *Always On My Mind: An exhibition in Aid of The National Brain Appeal*, at the Fitzrovia Gallery, London, July 2022.

Richard published the punk fanzine *Kick*. Five issues between 1979 and 1982.

He has written for: BBC (staff Features Writer), *NME* (pen name Richard North), ZigZag, *Offbeat* magazine, the *Guardian*, the *Daily Telegraph*, the *Independent*, *Artists & Illustrators* magazine, *The First Post*, *The Big Issue*, *3AM Magazine* (also an editor), London Arts Board/Arts Council England, *Siren* magazine, *Time Out*, *Cold Lips*, *International Times.*

His poem *Stolen Kisses* was published in *An Anthology of Punk Ass Poetry...* (Orchideater Press, 2022). Other poetry was published in various poetry magazines/websites.

Several of Richard's plays were performed at various theatres in London and nationwide, including the Arts Theatre, Covent Garden, London, Bread and Roses Theatre, Clapham, the Lost Theatre, Battersea, etc.

He was the bassist in the band Brigandage, writing/playing on the releases *FYM* (FO Records, 1984) and *Pretty Funny Thing* (Gung Ho Records, 1986). Track, *Angel of Vengeance,* is featured on the *Silhouettes and Statues* compilation CD (Cherry Red, 2017).

And Richard wrote the words to and performed the title track of the Necessary Animals' *Unkempt Magic* album (Yellow Fish Records, 2022)

He was a Visiting Lecturer in Contextual Studies (design and theory), University of East London, 2021.

richardcabut.com

✕

ENDNOTES

1   Mere Christianity by C.S. Lewis, published 1942. A collection of Lewis' broadcasts, compiled from his three previous books The Case for Christianity, Christian Behaviour, and Beyond Personality.

2   From a 2013 speech as related in Hermoine Lee biography Tom Stoppard: A Life (2020). (referenced for example : https://slate.com/culture/2021/02/tom-stoppard-life-biography-hermione-lee.html)

3   Coetzee makes this point a number of times, eg Notebook 1 to Waiting for the Barbarians, 1977, and here his interview with David Attwell in Doubling the Point: Essays and Interviews - J.M. Coetzee, Editor David Attwell (1992)

4   The Diary of Virginia Woolf, as described by Brian Dillon in In the Dark Room (2005)

Richard Cabut

Looking for a Kiss